ACCLAIM FOR A CLASSIC TALE OF FUTURE WAR

FINAL BLACKOUT

BY

L. RON HUBBARD

"Crackles with energy and bite . . .
a chilling prophecy for our time."

GREG DINALLO

author of "Rockets' Red Glare"

"A chilling and lucid picture
of the effects of incessant warfare."

KIRKUS REVIEWS

"A damn good story!"

JERRY POURNELLE

"Compelling . . . riveting . . . Hubbard's best.

PUBLISHERS WEEKLY

FINAL BLACKOUT

L. RON HUBBARD

London

Thames River

Sheerness

E N G L A N D

N

ENGLISH CHANNEL

Southeast England & Northwest Europe

Route to G.H.Q.
●●●●●●●●●●●●●●●●●●●●

Route to London

Kilometers 0 10 20 30 40 50 Km.

Statute Miles 0 10 20 30 40 50 Mi.

The Thames Estuary

Route to London

Kilometers
Statute Miles

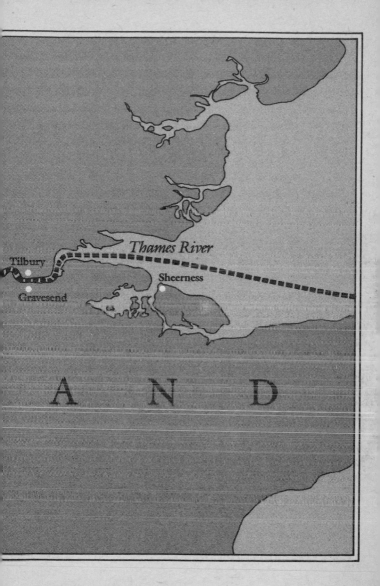

AMONG THE MANY CLASSIC WORKS
BY L. RON HUBBARD

Battlefield Earth
Beyond the Black Nebula
Buckskin Brigades
The Conquest of Space
The Dangerous Dimension
Death's Deputy
The Emperor of the Universe
Fear
Forbidden Voyage
The Incredible Destination
The Kilkenny Cats
The Kingslayer
The Last Admiral
The Magnificent Failure
The Masters of Sleep
The Mutineers
Ole Doc Methuselah
Ole Mother Methuselah

Mission Earth Vol. 1, The Invaders Plan
Mission Earth Vol. 2, Black Genesis
Mission Earth Vol. 3, The Enemy Within
Mission Earth Vol. 4, An Alien Affair
Mission Earth Vol. 5, Fortune of Fear
Mission Earth Vol. 6, Death Quest
Mission Earth Vol. 7, Voyage of Vengeance
Mission Earth Vol. 8, Disaster
Mission Earth Vol. 9, Villainy Victorious
Mission Earth Vol. 10, The Doomed Planet

The Rebels
Return to Tomorrow
Slaves of Sleep
To The Stars
The Traitor
Triton
Typewriter in the Sky
The Ultimate Adventure
The Unwilling Hero

FINAL BLACKOUT

L. RON HUBBARD

BRIDGE PUBLICATIONS, INC. LOS ANGELES

First Edition
10 9 8 7 6 5 4 3 2 1

Library of Congress Cataloging in Publication Data

Hubbard, L. Ron (Lafayette Ron), 1911 - 1986
    Final blackout
    1. Fiction, American. I. Title
    ISBN 0-88404-651-6 (alk. paper)

---

*To the men and officers
with whom I served
in World War II,
first phase, 1941-1945.*

Introduction

*F*inal Blackout is an extraordinary novel featuring an extraordinary hero—"The Lieutenant." The Lieutenant is unforgettable.

Fictional heroes come and go constantly in literature. They do their brave deeds, save the world, and usually are displaced by the next hero on the bookshelves.

In real life, the history of the world shows that mere victory is not what makes the memorable leader. George Washington is not honored for winning battles—he lost more than he won—but for establishing an enduring free republic in a world which up to then was almost totally ruled by rigid aristocracies. Winston Churchill fought for Britain in combat as a young man, but that isn't why he's a pivotal figure in the outcome of World War II ... or what most people think was its outcome. And

Mahatma Gandhi, who never fired a shot, then defeated Churchill's victorious British Empire and thus changed the course of history.

More than anything else *Final Blackout* offers importance. Under its fast-paced scenes of combat, passions, treachery and grim endurance in a war that never stopped, is its carefully developed, totally authentic portrait of The Lieutenant not as soldier but as strategist. Not as a merely military strategist—though to the end he sticks to his guns—but as a statesman. There's plenty of adventure in this book. But what The Lieutenant's spectacular career embodies is a down-to-basics description of why the world can be changed, why it only rarely changes for the better, and what that can mean for you and me. The book is populated by characters who would have been historical figures in what we call the real world. But as depicted in *Final Blackout,* their struggles for power hit sharply home to those of us who usually just have to put up with whatever history is doing to us whenever it wants to.

That's why this book and its hero have never been obscured since its first publication in a magazine, why many thousands have been reading various small editions of it over the years, why it's famous among those readers, and why this new large-audience edition was created in response to added thousands who had heard of it and wanted it. Like The Lieutenant, it's an "unkillable."

Its author is an extraordinary person. L. Ron Hubbard (1911–1986) wrote it during that strange, brief era when the then–Prime Minister of England was still issuing assurances of "peace in our time" and Hitler and Stalin, surely the two most numerically successful killers in history, were temporarily dividing up Europe preparatory to falling on each other. *Final Blackout* reached its first publication, as a three-part serial in a magazine called *Astounding Science Fiction.* By then, its author was within months of going off to fight in what some call World War II, what others see as the inevitable continuation of World War I, and which some can reasonably claim has never really come to a conclusion.

Astounding was the leading science fiction magazine of its day, propelled into prominence among those readers by a remarkable gathering of fresh new creative talents. L. Ron Hubbard was among the earliest of those, and in their first rank. Unlike his contemporaries—who would eventually include Robert A. Heinlein, Isaac Asimov, A. E. van Vogt, and many other authors who are still legendary names in that field and beyond it—Hubbard already had a powerful reputation in scores of popular fiction genres.

Years before his appearances in science fiction, he had begun as an adventure-story writer, and had then branched out to publish millions of words across almost the entire spectrum of newsstand fiction in its heyday. He was specifically brought in to lend the weight of his byline to the struggling *Astounding,* by its new publishers. Sales figures had convinced them L. Ron Hubbard's name on a magazine cover attracted thousands of added readers.

He quickly proved he could successfully transfer that magic to science fiction, and to fantasy in the sister publication *Unknown.* For his speed and productivity, and most important for his ability to deliver story after story that brought readers flocking, he almost overnight became a legend among legends. Some of his fellow authors even wrote stories in which he figured as a leading character, under thin disguises. All of them speak of him as a commanding figure, magnetic and full of gusto, standing at center-stage wherever these writers gathered in what has become known as the "Golden Age" of science fiction. He was a proven veteran of what was called "fictioneering," while most of them were yet novices . . . and he was still in his twenties.

He was 28 when he wrote *Final Blackout.* He had already been the author of scores of impressive shorter pieces in the field, making himself swiftly at home in it. He had often demonstrated the ability to pioneer fresh approaches to this literature. But even for him, and even for *Astounding,* his first novel in that medium was a stunner.

A Preface he wrote for a postwar small-press book edition is reprinted here following this Introduction. It conveys the sense of the immediate reaction among science fiction readers and then the spreading shockwaves of response from well beyond the boundaries of that readership.

With typical ironic humor, Hubbard "apologizes" for his naivete in world politics and his "youthful ignorance" of the high ideals that actually govern the leaders of society. As a satirical commentary, that Preface all by itself would make this book well worth attention. Almost uniquely among his mid-century writings, it conveys the tone of his ultimate science fiction magnum opus, the ten-volume *Mission Earth* novel of the 1980s. In its own way, it's rife with uncomfortably prophetic overtones as *Final Blackout* is in its way. The "young," "naive" L. Ron Hubbard had a disturbingly apt way of cutting through the pretensions of those who claimed to know best. The novel by the man who was readying himself for a major war was provocative reading, infuriating to some. So is the Preface produced six years later by the man fresh from that war . . . or from a major episode in that continuing war . . . and no less clear-eyed about what the future held.

It could easily be argued that *Final Blackout* did not belong in the pages of a "mere" science fiction magazine. Part of the initial impact on *Astounding*'s readers must have arisen from its expertise in military tactics, its confident grasp of strategy and, beyond that, of the chicaneries behind making war in search of political power.

Other writers in the field could write convincingly of "future war"; Hubbard's novel, however, had the ring of extra truth in countless details that none of his contemporaries could display. What's more, it was written from a level of political sophistication that was not hinted at again in speculative literature until George Orwell's postwar *Nineteen Eighty-Four* . . . a work which, of course, was too "serious" to first appear as a "mere" magazine serial. (Frankly, Hubbard's offering of an optimistic solution seems preferable to Orwell's cumulatively hopeless list of reasons why no solution is really possible.)

The answer to how the "young" Hubbard was able to bring this off is that he was uncommonly sophisticated and sharply educated in the best senses of those terms. Even when he began writing his earliest adventure stories, those were not based on armchair research but on personal experience in the wilder corners of the world. That experience in turn had been directed by his lifelong enthusiasm for learning new things and meeting new people, and trying out their ways himself.

Lafayette Ronald Hubbard was born in Nebraska but spent his earliest years in Montana, which even in the 1980s is still a place happily removed from many aspects of urban culture. In 1911, it was frontier in all but name. He was raised at first by his grandparents, his father being a U.S. Naval officer on duty, and it's said he could ride before he could walk. Early in the second decade of his life he was both an Eagle Scout and a blood-brother to the Blackfeet Indian Nation. His first hard-cover novel, *Buckskin Brigades*, 1937, would graphically depict the ruinous impact of early fur-trading incursions on the Blackfeet. (On its recent republication in the Bridge edition, the Blackfeet Tribal Council addressed a letter of gratitude to his spirit.) (As the youngest Eagle Scout in the nation, Hubbard was introduced at the White House and made friends with the son of President Calvin Coolidge.)

Shortly thereafter, under the direction of his father and his father's connections, Hubbard in his teens began traveling beyond the borders of the U.S., studying formally and informally with a variety of experts in human psychology, engineering and the sciences, while getting ample opportunity to observe how the world works in places as diverse as China and the Caribbean.

In addition to then going on to sail expeditions into places in both hemispheres that were then considered exotic—and some of which still are—he became a member of The Explorers Club. On several occasions he carried on expeditions under their flag, becoming an expert on Alaskan waters and charting them. There are some indications that his private and quasi-private small-vessel activities in that area extended along the Aleutian Islands and southwestward, just as there are strong indications that he was being groomed and was grooming himself for something special in the way of Naval service. So there is good reason to believe in Hubbard's practical understanding of human nature, military lore, and political history. There is equally good justification for believing that the geopolitical concerns *Final Blackout* reflects were on his mind for practical reasons that went far beyond the needs of earning a living as a writer. Certainly, when he formally entered the U.S. Navy in mid-1941, prior to Pearl Harbor, he did so under the auspices of a carefully worded April 8, 1941, letter to President Franklin D. Roosevelt from Congressman Warren D. Magnusson, head of the Naval Affairs Committee in the House of Representatives.

Hubbard was at sea enroute to duties in the Orient when the Japanese launched the war that many in and out of the U.S. military had been quietly expecting for some time. His actual military career is only now being reconstructed from documents obtained under the Freedom of Information Act, and from the testimony of former crew members on various vessels he commanded. (He appears to have known very well how to lead men, inspiring uncommon devotion and lifelong loyalty.)

He was also the Senior Naval Officer Present in Australia, gathering and directing supplies to General MacArthur's defense of the Philippines, before transferring to the Atlantic Fleet. His friend, Naval Academy graduate Robert A. Heinlein, has declared that Hubbard convalesced at his home from serious injuries that do not appear on the record released by the U.S. Navy after the war.

And if the Preface is pointedly ironic, that may well be related to the fact that Hubbard immediately after the war severed his connections to the Navy and soon thereafter began a new career—signaled by the release of *Dianetics, The Modern Science of Mental Health*—whose stated goal is the achievement of a sane planet. The dry wit visible in the *Final Blackout* Preface may not be all there is to this. Underneath, there may be a far deeper bite occasioned by experience in which Hubbard discovered that what he had written about as speculative fiction was very much like something all too true.

The haunting quality of *Final Blackout* can't now be separated from suppositions of that kind. When it was written, for instance, passages in which U.S. Marines are called in to suppress heroes were unheard-of in popular fiction. When they appeared in that marketplace, combat Marines were always the ultimate symbol of virtuous strength, fighting only on the side of pure right. Hubbard as a deft technician of writing was well aware of the value of "going too far" just far enough to titillate science fiction readers. He may have been doing no more than that. On the other hand, Hubbard may already have had reason to understand—as more of us do today— that the goodness and bravery of individuals can sometimes be put to dubious uses in high-level power-games conducted by world leaders.

In the history of the world, there have been persons in leadership positions who have not thought things through as well as they might have. Nor have they always been able to direct matters even skillfully enough to achieve their short-sighted objectives. One of the traditional places where the price for that is paid is in the trenches where the common soldier has to crawl in simple self-preservation. Far less often is the price paid in the distant citadels of power, and even then it is normally paid in bloodless coin, limousines taking the henchmen away to minimum-security detentions or to exile in luxury.

Final Blackout may be taken as an allegory—a speculative work of science fiction that teases the mind by presenting a world that, oh, could be, oh, yes, sounds plausible, but, well, never actually happened as predicted.

But over forty-nine years, *Final Blackout* has never ended, and the future runs infinitely long from this moment on.

—Algis Budrys

The son of a career soldier/diplomat, Algis Budrys was born in Europe in 1931 and has been a highly regarded science fiction novelist and editor since the early 1950s. He currently acts as the co-ordinator in L. Ron Hubbard's Writers of The Future Contest and its associated programs for nurturing new talent. He has taught seminars at Michigan State University, Brigham Young, Pepperdine University, and Harvard. He is equally well known as an award-winning historian and critic of modern speculative fiction. For the Chicago *Sun-Times* Sunday book review section, he has long written a column on popular literature in general.

—The Publisher

FINAL BLACKOUT

L. RON HUBBARD

Preface

When FINAL BLACKOUT was written there was still a Maginot Line, Dunkirk was just another French coastal town and the Battle of Britain, the Bulge, Saipan, Iwo, V2s and Nagasaki were things unknown and far ahead in history. While it concerns these things, its action will not take place for many years yet to come and it is, therefore, still a story of the future though some of the "future" it embraced (about one-fifth) has already transpired.

When published in magazine form before the war it created a little skirmish of its own and, I am told, as time has gone by and some of it has unreeled, interest in it has if anything increased. So far its career has been most adventurous as a story. The "battle of FINAL BLACKOUT" has included loud wails from the Communists—who said it was pro-fascist (while at least one fascist has held it to be pro-Communist). Its premises have been called wild and unfounded on the one hand while poems (some of them very good) have been written about or dedicated to the Lieutenant. Meetings have been held to nominate to greatness while others have been called to hang the author in effigy (and it is a matter of record that the last at least was successfully accomplished).

The British would not hear of its being published there at the time it appeared in America, though Boston, I am told, remained neutral—for there is nothing but innocent slaughter in it and no sign of rape.

There are those who insist that it is all very bad and those who claim for it the status of immortality. And while it probably is not the worst tale ever written, I cannot bring myself to believe that FINAL BLACKOUT, as so many polls and such insist, is one of the ten greatest stories in its field ever written.

Back in those mild days when Pearl Harbor was a place you toured while vacationing at Waikiki and when every drawing room had its business man who wondered disinterestedly whether or not it *was* not possible to do business with Hitler, the anti-FINAL BLACKOUTISTS (many of whom, I fear, were Communists, whatever those are) were particularly irked by some of the premises of the tale.

Russia was, obviously, a peace-loving nation with no more thought than America of entering the war. England was a fine, going concern without a thought, beyond a contemptuous aside, for the Socialist who, of course, could never come to power. One must understand this to see why FINAL BLACKOUT slashed about and wounded people.

True enough, some of its premises were far off the mark. It supposed, for instance, that the politicians of the great countries, particularly the United States, would push rather than hinder the entrance of the whole world into the war. In fact, it supposed, for its author was very young, that politicians were entirely incompetent and would not prevent for one instant the bloodiest conflict the country had ever known.

Further, for the author was no military critic, it supposed that the general staffs of most great nations were composed of stupid bunglers who would be looking at their mirrors when they should be looking to their posts and that the general worldwide strategy of war would go off in a manner utterly unadroit to the sacrifice of quite a few lives. It surmised that if general staffs went right on bungling along, nations would cease to exist, and it further—and more to the point—advanced the thought that the junior officer, the noncom and, primarily the enlisted man would have to prosecute the war. These, it believed, would finally be boiled down, by staff stupidity, to a handful of unkillables who would thereafter shift for themselves.

FINAL BLACKOUT dealt rather summarily— and very harshly, for the author was inexperienced in international affairs—that the anarchy of nations was an unhealthy arrangement maintained by the greed of a few for the privileges of a few and that the "common people" (which is to say those uncommon people who wish only to be let go about their affairs of getting enough to eat and begetting their next generation) would be knocked flat, silly and completely out of existence by these brand-new "defensive" weapons which would, of course, be turned only against soldiers. Bombs, atomics, germs and, in short, science, it maintained, were being used unhealthily and that, soon enough, a person here and there who was no party to the front line sortie was liable to get injured or dusty; it also spoke of populations being affected boomerang fashion by weapons devised for their own governments to use.

Certainly all this was heresy enough in that quiet world of 1939, and since that time, it is only fair to state, the author has served here and there and has gained enough experience to see the error of his judgment. Everything, it can be said with Pangloss, so far has been for the best in this best of all possible worlds.

There have been two or three stories modeled on *FINAL BLACKOUT.* I am flattered. It is just a story. And as the past few years proved, it cannot possibly happen.

L. RON HUBBARD
Hollywood, 1948

The Lieutenant

He was born in an air-raid shelter—and his first wail was drowned by the shriek of bombs, the thunder of falling walls and the coughing chatter of machine guns raking the sky.

He was taught in a countryside where A was for Antiaircraft and V was for Victory. He knew that Vickers Wellington bombers had flown non-stop clear to China. But nobody thought to tell him about a man who had sailed a carrack as far in the opposite direction—a chap called Columbus.

War-shattered officers had taught him the arts of battle on the relief maps of Rugby. Limping sergeants had made him expert with rifle and pistol, light and heavy artillery. And although he could not conjugate a single Latin verb, he was graduated as wholly educated at fourteen and commissioned the same year.

His father was killed on the Mole at Kiel. His uncle rode a flamer in at Hamburg. His mother, long ago, had died of grief and starvation in the wreckage which had been London.

When he was eighteen he had been sent to the front as a subaltern. At twenty-three he was commanding a brigade.

In short, his career was not unlike that of any other high-born English lad born after the beginning of that conflict which is sometimes known as the War of Books—or the War of Creeds, or the War Which Ended War or World Wars two, three, four and five. Like any other, with the exception that he lived through it.

There is little accounting for the reason he lived so long, and, having lived, moved up to take the spotlight on the Continental stage for a few seconds out of time. But there is never any accounting for such things.

When officers and men, sick with the hell of it, walked out to find a bullet that would end an unlivable life, he shrugged and carried on. When his messmates went screaming mad from illness and revulsion, he gave them that for which they begged, sheathed his pistol and took over the fragments of their commands. When outfits mutinied and shot their officers in the back, he squared his own and, faced front, carried on.

He had seen ninety-three thousand replacements come into his division before he had been a year on the Continent. And he had seen almost as many files voided over again.

He was a soldier and his trade was death, and he had seen too much to be greatly impressed with anything. Outwardly he was much like half a million others of his rank; inwardly there was a difference. He had found out, while commanding ack-acks in England, that nerves are more deadly than bullets, and so he had early denied the existence of his own, substituting a careless cheerfulness which went strangely with the somber gloom which overhung the graveyard of Europe. If he had nerves, he kept them to himself. And what battles he fought within himself to keep them down must forever go unsung.

Before he had been a year on the Continent, the dread soldier's sickness—that very learned and scientific result of bacteriological warfare, the climax of years of mutating germs unto final, incurable diseases—had caused a quarantine to be placed on all English troops serving across the Channel, just as America, nine years before, had completely stopped all communication across the Atlantic, shortly after her abortive atom war had boomeranged. Hence, he had not been able to return to England.

If he longed for his own land, shell-blasted though it might be, he never showed it. Impassively he had listened each time to the tidings of seven separate revolutions which had begun with the assassination of the king, a crime which had been succeeded by every known kind of political buffoonery

3

culminating in Communism (for at least that is what they called this ideology, though Marx would have disowned it. And the late, unlamented Stalin would have gibbered incoherently at the heresy of its tenets). And he saw only mirth in the fact that, whereas the crimson banner flew now over London, the imperial standard of the czar now whipped in the Russian breeze.

Seven separate governments, each attacked and made to carry on the war. Nine governments in Germany in only eighteen years. He had let the ribbons and insignia issued him drop into the mud, wishing with all his kind that all governments would collapse together and put an end to this. But that had never happened. The fall of one side netted attack from the organized other. And turn about. Just as the problem of manufacture had unequalized the periods of bombing, so had this served to prolong this war that the brief orgy of atomics, murderously wild, if utterly indecisive, had spread such hatreds that the lingering sparks of decency and forbearance seemed to have vanished from the world. War, as in days of old, had become a thing of hate and loot, for how else was a machine-tooled country to get machines and tools which it could no longer generate within itself.

He knew nothing about these international politics—or at least pretended that he did not. He was, however, in close touch with the effects, for such a collapse was always followed by the general advance of the other side. The fall of his own immediate clique in command meant that he, as a soldier, would be attacked; the banishing of the enemies' chiefs caused him to attack in turn. But war, to him, was the only actuality, for rarely had he known of that thing of which men spoke dreamily and to which they gave the name "peace."

He had seen, in his lifetime, the peak and oblivion of flight, the perfection and extinction of artillery, the birth and death of nuclear physics, the end product of bacteriology, but only the oblivion, extinction, and death of culture.

It had been three years since he had heard an airplane throbbing overhead. As a child, to him they had been as common as birds, if a shade more deadly. They had flown fast and far and then when the crash of atom bombs in guided missiles had finally blotted out three quarters of the manufacturing centers of the world they had flown no more. For the airplane is a fragile thing which cannot exist without replacement parts, without complex fuels, without a thousand aids. Even the assembly of a thousand partly damaged ships into perhaps fifty that would fly did not give a nation more than a few months' superiority in the air. It was quiet, very quiet. The planes had gone.

Once great guns had rumbled along definite lines. But big guns had needed artfully manufactured shells, and when the centers of manufacture had become too disorganized to produce such a complex thing as a shell, firing had gradually sputtered out, jerkily reviving, but fainter each time until it ceased. For the guns themselves had worn out. And when infantry tactics came to take the place of the warfare of fortresses and tanks, those few guns which remained had, one by one, been abandoned, perforce, and left in ruins to a rapidly advancing enemy. This was particularly true of the smaller field guns which had hung on feebly to the last.

It had been four years since he had received his last orders by radio, for there were no longer parts for replacement. And though it was rumored that G.H.Q. of the B.E.F. had radio communication with England, no one could truly tell. It had been seven years since a new uniform had been issued, three years or more since a rank had been made for an officer.

His world was a shambles of broken townships and defiled fields, an immense cemetery where thirty million soldiers and three hundred million civilians had been wrenched loose from life. And though the death which had shrieked out of the skies would howl no more, there was no need. Its work was done.

Food supplies had diminished to a vanishing point when a power, rumored to have been Russia, had spread plant insects over Europe. Starvation had done its best to surpass the death lists of battle. And, as an ally, another thing had come.

The disease known as soldier's sickness had wiped a clammy hand across the slate of Europe, taking ten times as many as the fighting of the war itself. Death crept silently over the wastes of grass-grown shell holes and gutted cities, slipping bony fingers into the cogs of what organization had survived. From the Mediterranean to the Baltic, no wheel turned for the illness was not one disease germ grossly mutated into a killer which defied penicillin, sulfa, pantomecin, and stereo-rays, it was at least nine illnesses, each one superior to yellow fever or the bubonic plague. The nine had combined amongst themselves to create an infinite variety of manifestations. In far countries, South America, South Africa, Scandinavia, where smoke might have belched from busy chimneys, nearly annihilated nations which had never been combatants had closed their ports and turned to wooden sticks for plows. Their libraries might still bulge with know-how but who could go there to read them? Nations entirely innocent of any single belligerent move in this war, or these many wars, had become, capitals and hamlets alike, weed-grown and tumbled ruins to be quarantined a half century or more from even their own people.

But the lieutenant was not unhappy about it. He had no comparisons. When lack of credit and metal and workmen had decreed the abandonment of the last factory, he had received the tidings in the light that artillery had never accomplished anything in tactics, anyway, Napoleon to the contrary. When the last rattling wreck of a plane had become a rusting pile of charred metal, he had smiled his relief. What had planes done but attack objectives they could not hold.

From the records which remain of him, it is difficult to get an accurate description of the man himself, as difficult as it is easy to obtain minute accounts of his victories and defeats. His enemies represent him as having an upsetting and even ghoulish way of smiling, an expression of cheerfulness which never left him even when he meted death personally. But enemies have a way of distorting those they fear, and the oft-repeated statement that he took no pleasure in anything but death is probably false.

Such a view seems to be belied by the fact that he took no pleasure in a victory unless it was bloodless so far as his own troops were concerned. This may be accounted as a natural revulsion toward the school of warfare which measured the greatness of a victory in terms of its largeness of casualty lists. Incredible as it may seem, even at the time of his birth, the mass of humanity paid no attention to strategic conquests if they were not attended by many thousands of deaths. But men, alas, had long since ceased to be cheap, and the field officer or staff officer that still held them so generally died of a quiet night with a bayonet in his ribs. And so the question may be argued on both sides. He might or might not be credited with mercy on the score that he conserved his men.

Physically, he seems to have been a little over medium height, blue-gray of eye and blond. Too, he was probably very handsome, though we only touch upon his conquests in another field. The one picture of him is a rather bad thing, done by a soldier of his command after his death with possibly more enthusiasm than accuracy.

He may have had nerves so high-strung that he was half mad in times of stress—and not unlikely, for he was intelligent. He might have educated himself completely out of nerves. As for England herself, he might have loved her passionately and have done those things he did all for her. And, again, it might have been a cold-blooded problem in strategy which it amused him to solve.

These things, just as his name, are not known. He was the lieutenant. But whether he was madman and sadist or gentleman and patriot—this must be solved by another.

Chapter I

The brigade huddled about two fires in the half dawn, slowly finishing off a moldy breakfast, washing down crumbs of rotted bread with drafts of watery, synthetic tea. About them stood the stark skeletons of a forest, through the broken branches of which crept wraiths of mist, quiet as the ghosts of thirty million fighting men.

Half-hidden by the persistent underbrush were several dark holes; down awry steps lay the abandoned depths of a once-great fortress, garrisoned now by skeletons which mildewed at their rusty guns.

Though not yet wholly awake, the attitudes of the men were alert through long practice. Each man with half himself was intent upon each slightest sound, not trusting the sentries who lay in foxholes round about. Much of this tautness was habit. But more of it, today, had direction. A night patrol had brought word that several hundred Russians occupied the ridges surrounding this place. And the brigade which had once been six thousand strong now numbered but a hundred and sixty-eight.

They were a motley command: Englishmen, Poles, Spaniards, Frenchmen, Finns and Italians, uniformed in the rags of twenty nations, friend and foe alike. They were armed with a catalogue of weapons, the cartridges of one seldom serving the rifle of another. They were clothed and armed, then, by the whim and experience of each.

In common they had endless years of war behind them. In common they had the habit of war. Long since the peasants of the armies had slid over the hill, back to devastated farms and fields, leaving only those who had but one talent.

The English could not, because of the quarantine against soldier's sickness, go home. Once they had had sweethearts, wives and families. But no one had heard for so long—

They had survived whole divisions of replacements. They had been commanded by more officers than they could count. They had been governed by more creeds than they could ever understand.

Here was their world, a shattered wood, an empty fortress, a breakfast of crumbs and hot water, each man hard by his rifle, each existing for the instant and expecting the next to bring danger and death.

These were the unkillables, immune to bullets, bombs and bugs, schooled in war to perfection, kept alive by a seventh and an eighth sense of danger which could interpret the slightest change in their surroundings and preserve themselves from it.

Having lost all causes and connections, having forgotten their religions, they still had one god, their lieutenant. He was, after all, a highly satisfactory god. He fed them, clothed them and conserved their lives—which was more than any other god could have done.

Now and then eyes wandered to the lieutenant and were quieted by the sight of him. For, despite all danger, the lieutenant was sitting upon the half-submerged wheel of a caisson, shaving himself with the help of a mirror stuck in the crotch of a forked stick.

The cook came up with a kettle of hot water which he emptied into the old helmet which served the lieutenant as a washbasin. The cook was a corpulent fellow of rather murderous aspect, wholly unwashed and hairy and carrying a naked bayonet thrust through his belt.

"Can I get the leftenant anythin' else, sir?"

"Why, yes. A fresh shirt, an overcoat, a new pistol and some caviar."

"I would if them Russians had any, sir."

"I've no doubt of it, Bulger," smiled the lieutenant. "But, really, haven't you something a bit special for breakfast? This is an anniversary, you know.

My fifth year at the front was done yesterday."

"Congratulations, leftenant, sir. If you don't mind my mentioning it, are you goin' to start the sixth year with a fight?"

"Ho!" said a rough voice nearby. "You'll be advising us on tactics next. Stick to your foraging, Bulger." And Pollard, the sergeant major, gave the cook a shove back toward the fire. "Sir, I just toured the outposts and they been hearin' troops movin' on the high ground. Weasel is out there and he claims he heard gun wheels groanin' about four."

"Gun wheels!" said the lieutenant.

"That's what he said."

The lieutenant grinned and rinsed off his face. "Some day a high wind is going to catch hold of his ears and carry him off."

"About them Russians, sir," said Pollard, soberly, "are we just going to stay here until they close in on us? They know we're down here. I feel it. And them fires—"

Pollard was stopped by the lieutenant's grin. He was a conscientious sergeant, often pretending to a sense of humor which he did not possess. No matter how many men he had killed or how terrible he was in action, his rugged face white with battle lust, he shivered away from ridicule at the hands of the lieutenant. In his own way he respected the boy, never giving a thought that his officer was some twenty-three years his junior.

The lieutenant slid into his shirt and was about

to speak when the smallest whisper of a challenge sounded two hundred yards away. Instantly the clearing was deserted, all men instinctively taking cover from which they could shoot with the smallest loss of life and the greatest damage to the foe. There had been a note of anxiety in that challenge.

The lieutenant, pistol in hand, stood with widespread boots, playing intelligent eyes through the misty woods. A bird call sounded and the camp began to relax, men coming back to their fires and again addressing their synthetic tea.

After a little, as the call had indicated, an English officer strode through the underbrush, looked about and then approached the lieutenant. Although a captain, he was dressed in no manner to indicate his outfit. Like the lieutenant, he had amalgamated the uniforms of some four services into an outfit which was at least capable of keeping out the wet.

"Fourth Brigade?" he questioned.

"Right," said the lieutenant. "Hello, Malcolm."

The captain looked more closely and then smiled and shook the extended hand. "Well, well! I never expected to find you, much less get to you. By the guns, fellow, did you know these ridges are alive with Russians?"

"I suspected so," said the lieutenant. "We've been waiting three days for them."

Malcolm started. "But . . . but here you are, in a death trap!" He covered his astonishment. "Well!

I can't presume to advise a brigade commander in the field."

"You've come from G.H.Q.?"

"From General Victor, yes. I had the devil's own time getting to you and then finding you. I say, old boy, those Russians—"

"How is General Victor?"

"Between us, he's in a funk. Ever since the British Communist Party took over London and executed Carlson, Victor hasn't slept very well."

"Bulger," said the lieutenant, "bring the captain some breakfast."

Bulger lumbered up with a whole piece of bread and a dixie of tea which the staff officer seized upon avidly.

"Not much," said the lieutenant, "but it's the last of the supplies we found cached here in this fortress. Eat slowly, for the next, if any, will have to be Russian. Now. Any orders?"

"You're recalled to G.H.Q. for reorganization."

The lieutenant gave a slight quiver of surprise. "Does this have anything to do—with my failure to comply with the B.C.P. Military Committee's orders to appoint soldiers' councils?"

Malcolm shrugged and spoke through a full mouth and without truth. "Oh, no. Who'd bother about that? I think they wish to give you a wider command. They think well of you, you know."

"Then—" said the lieutenant, knowing full well that a recalled officer was generally a deposed officer.

"It's the general's idea. But, see here, those Russians—"

"I'll engage them shortly," said the lieutenant. "They're fresh and they ought to have boots and bread and maybe something to drink. My favorite listening post, a chap named Weasel, said he heard wheels last night."

"Right. I was going to tell you. I saw a trench mortar and an antitank rocket—"

"No!"

"Truth," said Malcolm.

"Artillery!"

"No less."

"Well, I'll — Why, there hasn't been a field piece on this front since the storming of Paris two years ago. Though mortars and bazookas could hardly be called field pieces. Have they got shells, do you suppose?"

"They had caissons."

"And—say! Horses!"

"I saw two!"

The lieutenant beamed happily. "Ah, you've come just in time. Roast horse. Think of it! Brown, sizzling, dripping, juicy horse!"

"Horse?" said Bulger, instantly alert although he had been a hundred feet and more away.

The brigade itself looked hopeful; they moved about through the naked starkness of the trees and tried to catch sight of the Russians on the heights.

The event was, to say the least, unusual. And

the thought of food momentarily clogged Malcolm's wits. In light of what he was trying to do, he would never have made such a statement. "It's been a long time since I've had a decent meal of anything. Much less horse."

The lieutenant caught at the remark. There was no sympathy between field officers and staff officers, for, while the former fought and starved, the latter skulked in the protection of impregnable G.H.Q. and received occasional rations from England, existing between times on condensed food stored in times past for many more men than were now left alive. That a staff officer had risked this trek in the first place struck the lieutenant as being very odd.

"What's up?"

Malcolm realized then, possibly from the sharpness of the tone, that he had done wrong.

"What's up?" repeated the lieutenant insistently.

Malcolm put a good face on it. "I shouldn't tell you, but we're out of touch with England. There's been no food for three months."

"That isn't all you can tell me."

Malcolm squirmed. "Well, if you'll have it. G.H.Q. is recalling all field troops. General Victor is thinking of withdrawing from our present base into the south where there may be some fertile area. It will be better for all of us." Sycophant that he was, he sought to allay further questioning. "I was sent expressly to get you. Your ability is well known and appreciated, and Victor feels that, with you guiding operations, we cannot fail."

The lieutenant brushed it aside. "You're telling me that England—no, not England but those damned Communists there—have forbidden us ever to return."

"Well—the quarantine did that."

"But it left room for hope," said the lieutenant. Malcolm was silent.

"They're afraid," said the lieutenant. "Afraid we'll come back and turn their government appetite over dixie." He laughed sharply. "Poor little shivering fools! Why, there aren't ten thousand British troops left in the world outside of England. Not one man where there was once a thousand. We've battered French and German and Russian and Italian and German again until we're as few as they. First we came over to get machine tools and food. Then, with one excuse or another they began to tell us false tales of impending invasion but it has been two years since we could locate anything you could call a political entity on this continent. We can't go home because we'll take the sickness. And what are we here? We're mixed up with fifty nationalities, commanded by less than a hundred officers, scattered from Egypt to Archangel. Ten thousand men and ten million, twenty million graves. Outcasts, men without a country. A whole generation wiped out by shot and starvation and sickness and those that are left scarcely able to keep belly, ribs and jacket together. And they're afraid of us in England!"

It had its effect upon Malcolm. He had been out only two years. Sent originally full of hope and swagger with a message for General Victor from the supreme council and never afterwards allowed to return home. For a moment he forgot his fear of a field officer, remembering instead a certain girl, weeping on a dock. "I'll get back some way. It's not final. I'll see her again!"

"Not under Victor, you won't."

"Wait," cautioned Malcolm, afraid again. "He's your superior officer."

"Perhaps," and in that word Malcolm read direful things.

"But you'll obey him?" said Malcolm.

"And go back to G.H.Q.? Certainly."

Malcolm sighed a little with relief. How dull these field officers were at times! Didn't they ever hear anything? But then, thirty or more outfits had innocently obeyed that order, little knowing that they would be stripped of their commands immediately upon arrival and asked to be off and out of sight of the offended staff. But, no, the lieutenant would not understand until the whole thing was over. There was nothing unreasonable in this to Malcolm. Importance now was measured only by the number of troops an officer commanded. It was not likely that the staff would leave mutinous field officers at the head of soldiers and thus menace the very foundation of the general staff.

"They've had their way in England," said the lieutenant. "Yes. They've had their way."

Malcolm was troubled again. He quickly redirected the lieutenant's line of thought. "It will be all right when we have a new post. We'll carve out a large section of fertile country and there'll be food enough for all."

"Yes?" said the lieutenant.

Malcolm could read nothing from that at all. He shivered involuntarily, for he had heard strange tales from out of the darkness of the Continent.

"What's this?" said the lieutenant. "Fever? Carstone! Draw a drink off that Belgian alcohol machine gun and give it to Captain Malcolm."

"Thanks," said Malcolm, affected.

The lieutenant got up and stretched. To look at him one would not suspect that he had been starved his entire life, for his body was firm and healthy. He had been born into hardship and he had thrived upon it. He smoothed out his blond hair with his fingers and set an Italian duriron helmet upon his head. He shrugged into his tunic and buckled his belts. Out of habit he checked over his automatic, examining each bullet in the three clips.

Mawkey, a little fellow with a twisted spine and a set of diabolical eyes, who usually waited upon the lieutenant, came forward with a rag and wiped the lieutenant's boots. Then, from a broken limb he took down the bullet-proof cape which had been captured from a Swiss nearly four years ago. It was inch-thick silk, weighing almost thirty pounds in itself and weighted further by the slugs which had lodged in it and which could not be cut out without ruining it. Mawkey fastened it about the lieutenant's shoulders and then began to pack the shaving effects into a gas-mask container.

"Where have you been?" said the lieutenant.

"I took a personal scout," said Mawkey, pointing to his superfine eyes, the best in the brigade. He grinned evilly. "Russians begin to move about daylight; they creep down ravines toward here. I see officers on hummock up there." He pointed to an exposed hill. "See them?"

"No."

"Just a cap here and there."

"The officers, you say?"

"See! The sun hit a field glass!"

"I didn't but we'll take your word."

"Good Heaven, man," said Malcolm, "you're not just going to sit here and wait for them!"

"Why not? Would you have us charge across the open at men with artillery?"

"No, but—"

"Take it easy," said the lieutenant. "Sergeant, bring all but two posts in. Be ready to march in ten minutes."

"Yessir."

"March?" said Malcolm. "But where?"

A sentry came wriggling out of the brush and ran to the lieutenant. "I zee seex, seven Russian patrol come." And he pointed west.

And an instant later two more sentries came in breathlessly, pointing to the south and the east. The Russian post of command had already been indicated in the north.

"You're caught!" said Malcolm. "They've spotted you by your fires!"

"Bulger, throw on a few green sticks to make more smoke," replied the lieutenant. "Have you got all the wrong-caliber ammunition, Pollard?"

"And some from the fortress down there, sir."

"Good. Put a squad to work gathering all the dry wood in sight. Stand by to throw it on the fires. Carstone, better check your pneumatics."

"Yessir."

"Yessir."

"Tou-tou, stand by to head the rear guard and pick your men."

"Yess, yess, mon lieutenant."

"Good Heaven, old boy!" said Malcolm. "Of what use is a rear guard when there is nowhere to retreat? Oh, yes, I know. I'm steady. But every time I see one of you field officers preparing a defense or attack, I get a headache. You aren't according to the book, you know, not at all. I say, how fine it would be to have some artillery ourselves."

"Worthless stuff."

"Eh?"

"If I had an antitank rifle and a trench mortar, what would be the result? Lord, didn't they prove that years ago? One side cancels out the damage of the other by inflicting just as much. Chap called Napoleon brought artillery into style, or so these French tell me. Absolutely useless stuff except for pounding down a wall. As useless as airplanes. Too many casualties and grief for too little fun."

"Fun?"

"Why not? Herrero, give Bulger a hand with his kettles."

The camp was boiling with efficient activity. Carstone's crews were hard at work upon the pneumatic machine guns. Once they had been run by gasoline with the hand compressors as auxiliary. But now there was only the auxiliary. Four men were priming them to full load while Carstone checked their battered gauges. Born out of the problem that a machine gun is always located by its noise, the pneumatics had stayed to solve the problem of scanty ammunition, for they fired slugs salvaged from British issue in which the powder had decayed. And there were plenty of such dumps. They were mismatched weapons at best, for their carriages had been intended for ambitious supersonic weapons which had been designed to kill at five hundred yards. But these, when their condensers had failed and their batteries could not be replaced had long since become part of the European terrain, only the wheels and mounts surviving.

The lieutenant paced about the clearing, checking up, watching for the last posts to come in and the first Russian to appear.

And then the Weasel popped up, yelling, "Shell!"

An instant later everyone heard it and then saw it. It was a trench mortar, tumbling down the sky. Somebody, having pity for a man who had never seen one, bore Malcolm backward into cover of the caisson. The bomb struck and exploded, directly in the center of the clearing. Shrapnel screamed wickedly as it tore through the already maimed trees.

Chapter II

In that shower of death it seemed preposterous that any of the hundred and sixty-eight could have escaped, for the trench mortar was of very large caliber. But the fragments had barely ceased screaming when men again populated the clearing. A swift survey showed that only a kettle and a pack had suffered and the latter but slightly.

"Tou-tou!" said the lieutenant. "Take cover in that passage mouth to cover us."

"Yess, yess, mon lieutenant."

"Double file, follow me!" cried the lieutenant, striding to the top of the largest entrance of the fortress. At the top he paused. "All right. Quickly. Down with you." And he passed his hurrying men by him and below with a gesture.

A shrill piping, growing stronger, again cleared the place as though by magic. The three-pounder blazed out and shrapnel again hammered the wood. But the men were up and hurrying through its smoke before branches had ceased to fall.

"Pollard!" said the lieutenant.

"Yessir," replied the sergeant major.

"Give a hand. Get down below there, Malcolm. We're all right. All below, now."

With the sergeant's help the lieutenant began to pile the dry brush upon the fire. Mawkey, in the entrance, yelped, "Mortar!"

It burst almost on the fire.

The lieutenant and Pollard slipped out from behind cover and completed the piling of the brush. Then, with the boxes supported between them, they began to empty two hundred pounds of assorted and cast-off bullets through the brush pile. An old device it was, almost as old as cartridges themselves but oldest things are often the surest.

"Shell!" howled Mawkey.

The piping ended in a roaring flash. The top of a tree leaned slowly over and then plummeted to earth. The lieutenant, up again, pulled the glass visor of his Italian helmet down over his face and wrapped his cloak tightly about him.

"Get down with our people there!" he shouted to Pollard.

The sergeant was reluctant, but he obeyed. By now, because of the pauses caused by the shells, a few of the cartridges were beginning to explode in the brush pile. Slugs occasionally made the silk cloak whip up about the skirt. The lieutenant emptied the last box and dived down into the entrance.

Behind them a slow firing had commenced to mount in volume.

The lieutenant lifted his visor and thrust through the crowd which was huddled in the outer chamber. He raised his hand in the honored signal to follow him and plunged off along a corridor. The pavement was very uneven, broken up by roots. Here and there steel beams in the roof had rusted through to let down piles of rubble. About a hundred and twenty yards up the line they passed a barrack in which tier upon tier of collapsed bunks still held the skeletons of men who had been caught by the direct hit of a gas shell. Above, on another level, the twisted and corrosion-congealed remains of big guns stood like prehistoric monsters, forgotten by time.

From observation slots along the way, sheets of light came through, flicking along the passing column.

"I didn't know any of these were left," said Malcolm in an awed voice. "I'd heard about them being used once   How many dead there are here!"

"Fortress fever, mutinies— Toward the last, the pioneers had a trick of lowering gas grenades through the observation slots from above."

Malcolm tripped over a sprawled human framework and a shaft of light caught in the gold of medals as they tinkled down through the ribs. He hurried on after the lieutenant.

There were whispers about them as the few surviving rats hid from them; rats once bold enough to attack a sleeping man and tear out his eyes before he could awake.

The column moved quietly. Long ago they had discarded the last of their hobnails, for these had a habit of scraping against stones and giving a maneuver away. They kept no step or order of march, for each, as an individual, had his own concern, his own method of caring for himself, and so they strung out far. Even though it had been years since such a fortress had been garrisoned by any of them, they instinctively took precaution against direct hits on the tunnel roof above them.

The tunnel dipped and, for a little way, they sloshed knee-deep in water. Shaggy Corporal Carstone, in charge of the machine-gun company, clucked like a mother hen as he got his precious charges over the rough places; for while water could do no harm, the tanks were so worn and thin that one stumble might put them out of action, filled as they were with their full weight of air.

Now and then the lieutenant struck his flint to find a chalk mark on the wall and thus determine the right turn, and Malcolm began to realize that the place had been recently mapped. Malcolm, following the shadow of the cloak, was struck by the expression which each flint flash revealed upon the lieutenant's face. For the lieutenant had a twinkle in his eye and a sardonic smile upon his lips, as though he was hugely enjoying this business.

Malcolm's ear caught the sound of firing each time they passed an observation slot, and it began to come to him that the cartridge-filled brush was burning gradually, thus acting as a time fuse on the bullets. In truth it sounded as though the clearing far back was bitterly defended. He eyed the lieutenant with renewed respect. But for all that the lieutenant was not a known quantity to him. None of these scattered officers were. They seemed to be without nerves, impervious to all anxiety, able to subsist upon nothing. He had heard something of the officers of yesterday; how they had driven unwilling troops with a drawn pistol and a lash, how they had carried out the stupid orders which always led to slaughter against heavily fortified objectives. He had heard, too, that many an officer had been found with a bullet in his back. But that was yesterday, a yesterday a fifth of a century dead. A yesterday when prisoners had been shot to avoid giving them rations, when every slightest spark of gallantry had been swallowed in the barbaric lust of battle which had swept the Continent as madness might sweep through a pack of dogs.

It was not that the lieutenant was kind. He merely did not care. His men did not belong to a government but to himself; just as he belonged to them. It seemed that all men with nerves had died of them, leaving a strange corps of beings above such things as human weakness and death, men who had evolved for themselves a special art of living. Malcolm had no hopes for the mercies of the lieutenant; they did not exist. And he was thinking to himself, following that cape, that the race of fighting men, while laudable in many ways, had degenerated in others. Their love of battle was quite finished and bravery was a word. For what better evidence could he have than this fact of the lieutenant's running away from a force because it had field pieces?

A question annoyed Malcolm. They were outward bound from the last encampment. But had they any destination? What would they do for food?

Ahead a hazy blur of light became apparent. Weeds had choked the exit from the fortress, and the roof had fallen until it was necessary to crawl belly down on the rubble to get out.

The lieutenant made a cautious survey. Ahead stretched an indistinct trench which had once communicated with the rear. It had been dug in a sloping ravine which fell away to the north. They had come through the hill on which the Russians had established their P.C.

Stepping aside, the lieutenant passed his men out. Hardly a shrub waved to mark their presence in the trench. They did not group, but faded into cover until a very small space, apparently quite empty, actually contained the whole force.

"Pollard, take the east slope," whispered the lieutenant. "Tou-tou—where are you?"

"Here the same, mon lieutenant," said Tou-tou, crawling out.

"You waited for contact?"

"Yess, mon lieutenant. Zey are ssso young, so many."

"Very well. Take the west slope. Work up toward the crest and in one half hour by the sun you will hear our signal to attack. Carstone, wait here in case there is any firing from above and cover our retreat if necessary. If we are successful, come up quickly with your guns. Weasel, locate their baggage; take six men and be very quiet when you take the sentries."

"Right, sir."

"Pass the word. First Regiment with Pollard, Second with Tou-tou, Third with me. Remember, no firing, only wires, clubs and knives. And do not kill their commander or the staff."

The word was passed like a gentle draft of air. Then Pollard was gone and a third of the brigade melted away. Tou-tou's third vanished without a sound. The lieutenant thrust a stick into the earth to watch its shadow. The sun was still very low and the mist over the valleys had not wholly burned away. From over the ridge came the clatter of rifle fire and the occasional dull thump of grenades.

Presently the lieutenant signaled with his hand and slid out of the trench and through the underbrush toward the crest. Malcolm stayed by Carstone.

Spread thin, the Third Regiment slithered silently upward. They could not yet see the crest, for the way was long and there were several false ridges. This hillside was very uneven, pock-marked with shell holes now very indistinct. Everywhere before the advance, rabbits scurried and dived into cover. They were avoided by the soldiers for the reason that they carried a deadly sickness, and though all were probably immune, it was not good to take chances. Only the birds with which the Continent now teemed were good prey, but the soldiers were so nauseated by their meat by now that they seldom took the trouble to set snares.

A squeal, scarcely started before it was stopped, told of some providential soul picking up a pig of the type which had long forgotten its domestication. These were too rare to be overlooked, but First Sergeant Hanley, a tough Scot nominally commanding the Third Regiment, went slipping off on a tangent to reprimand the act.

Mawkey, who had scuttled ahead, came back now, his evil eyes bright with excitement. "They all face south. There are about six officers and a guard of thirty soldiers. The artillery is over to your right in an old field-gun emplacement."

"Gian," whispered the lieutenant to an Italian sergeant with a perpetually hungry look, "take a company over and stand ready to squash the gunners between Tou-tou and yourself when he comes up."

"Si," bobbed Gian. "I hope they have rations."

"Who ever heard of a Russian who had anything to eat?" said the lieutenant. "On your way."

Gian was there and then wasn't there. Aside from the distant firing, there was no sound. The battery above had ceased to bellow some time ago, being uncertain of the positions of its own troops.

The lieutenant glanced at the sun and then thrust another stick into the center of a flat place and measured the shadow with the spread of his hand just to be sure. He had three or four minutes left of the half-hour. He pulled down the visor over his face and the men near him did the same. There was a slight snicking sound as firing mechanisms were checked and bayonets tested.

More slowly now the lieutenant brought them forward. Mawkey, at his side, was trembling with eagerness as he unrolled his favorite weapon—a stick to which was attached three lengths of light chain appended by choicely sharp chunks of shrapnel.

They were almost to the crest now, so flat in the tall grass that they were still invisible to the Russians. The lieutenant checked the sun. He whistled the trill of a meadow lark three times, paused and then whistled it again.

There was a yelp of terror, hacked off short, over by the battery. A second later the grass all about the P.C. erupted with soldiers. A Russian officer emitted a hysterical string of commands and the thirty men whirled about to be drowned in a sea of charging men. Two or three guns went off. The crew of an alcohol machine gun valiantly tried to slew about their weapon and then, seeing it was no use, tossed down their sidearms.

The commander was a young man of very severe aspect. He started to roar his complaint and then, seeing a way out, leaped toward the lip of the ridge. Mawkey's weapon wrapped about his legs and he went down. Ruefully he disentangled the weapon and began to massage his shins.

It was all over before the dust had had a chance to rise. Thirty prisoners, one slightly wounded, were disarmed. Tou-tou came up with the battery crew and reported that Gian was manning the field pieces, which were six, not two.

"No casualties," reported Tou-tou, grinning.

Pollard, who had been a little tardy, thanks to an unforeseen ravine, was cross. A runner came up from the Weasel to report that all baggage was in hand, but that the Russians had surrendered upon seeing themselves outpointed.

The lieutenant took off his visored helmet, for it was very hot in the sun, and handed it with his cloak to Mawkey, taking the remnant of a British flying cap in return. Now that the Russian commander had regained his composure, the lieutenant called attention to him with a bow.

"I am indebted to you, sir."

The commander, who spoke fair English, bowed in his turn. "I have been outmaneuvered, sir. I congratulate you."

"Thank you. Now hadn't we better recall your troops before they squander all their ammunition on a pile of brush filled with bullets?"

The commander blinked and then recovered, smiling. "So that was the trick."

"That is the center of an old fortress system," said the lieutenant.

"I did not know the region."

"Which could hardly be expected. We waited for you for three days."

"I apologize for my underestimate of the troops here. We were sent out some three months ago to carve our way through to the sea and inspect the region in the hope that food can be shipped inland from here."

"There is no food," said the lieutenant. "In fact, if you can forgive such sentiment, we attacked you solely because we were informed you had horses."

"Ah," said the commander, understanding. He turned and rattled an order to an aide who stood by to hoist a recall flag upon further command.

"About the terms," said the commander, "I trust that you follow the custom of these days."

"All prisoners disarmed and released and all impersonal baggage retained."

"Sir, although I dislike having to ask further forbearance from a man I respect, I hope you will allow us to retain our arms. The country through which we have passed is filled with roving bands of soldiers."

"Of course, you will give me your parole," said the lieutenant, "and swear on your honor as an officer to return to your center of government?"

"Certainly. You, perhaps, can give me the data we wish."

"Certainly. And now pardon me. Pollard, man that alcohol gun and send word to our battery to stand by. Have Weasel bring up the baggage train to that ravine below there. Your troops," he said, turning back to the commander, "will be left in possession of their rifles and ammunition. We shall retain the battery and animals and all impersonal baggage."

"Thank you," said the commander, giving the signal to hoist the recall. "We shall begin our return at noon. You wish my troops to remain there in the valley, of course, until they march?"

"Naturally."

"And you say there is no fertile region between here and the sea?"

"On my honor I know of none. England has exhausted herself and is of no value, and I dare say your own country is in like condition."

"Well— Sir, may I be frank?"

"Of course."

"We were not sent anywhere. We are the last of the Imperial White Russian Army which was defeated and thrown out of Moscow five months ago. The new government, I believe, strictly favored isolation and, I am certain, is in no position to favor anything else. There is no government now in Germany, aside from a few scattered officers in places which were not touched by the many waves of crop-destroying insects and disease bacteria. Spheres of isolation are being formed with scorched-earth belts about them. We sought to establish ourselves in Paris, some two weeks' march from here, but there is nothing there but starvation. We sought to reach the coast in the hope that the starvation frontiers had not yet reached there."

"They have."

"For your sake I regret it."

"Where shall you go now?"

"I am not sure, but I am told by stray wanderers that there may be such regions in Italy. We have been living as we could off the land, and we can continue to do so. We seem to be wholly immune to soldier's sickness and for that we are thankful. A serum was developed in Moscow last year and we have all been given it."

"I trust you find such a place in Italy," said the lieutenant, extending his hand.

"And luck to you," said the Russian. He bowed and turned on his heel, marching at the head of his staff and bodyguard down to the waiting troops in the valley below. With them went their own belongings.

The lieutenant watched from his vantage spot for some time and then, regaining his good spirits, made a tour of his brigade, pleased as any commander should be when he has chosen his ground, carried through an elementary bit of strategy and tactics and found that his men still behaved well.

That afternoon, with the Russians gone, the lieutenant's forces tasted the fruits of victory. One and all, they gorged themselves upon dripping roasts of horseflesh, cooked by a prideful Bulger.

Chapter III

For eight days the Fourth Brigade lived off the Russians. It was not luxurious, but it was better than crumbs scraped out of a fortress twenty years in its grave. Apparently the Russians had met and defeated other forces to the east, for the stores included a kind of bread, made of bark and wild wheat, peculiar to Rumanian troops and a wine which Alsatian soldiers concocted from certain roots. Too, there were some spare tunics and overcoats, evidently located in some hitherto-forgotten dump. These, though slightly moldy and insect-frayed, were most welcome, especially since they were light tan, a color which blended well with the autumn which was upon them.

But at the end of eight days the brigade began to show signs of restlessness. Wild geese, in increasing flocks, had begun to wing southward, and the men lay on their backs, staring moodily into the blue, idly counting.

The lieutenant paced along a broken slab of concrete which had once been part of a pillbox commanding the valley. For, with the new guns and even the scarce ammunition, the troops did not need to fear sunlight.

In his ears, too, sounded the honking which heralded an early winter. And the caterpillars which inched along and tumbled off the guns had narrow tan ruffs which clearly stated that the winter would be a hard one. Spiders, too, confirmed it.

It was one of those infrequent times when the lieutenant did not smile, which heightened the effect of his seriousness. Men moved quietly when they came near and did not linger but cat-footed away. The battery crew silently sat along the grass-niched wall and studiously regarded their boots, only glancing up when the lieutenant went the other way.

All hoped they knew what he was thinking. The winter past had not been a comfortable one: starving, they had huddled in an all-but-roofless church, parsimoniously munching upon the stores they had found buried there—stores which had not lasted through. At that time the Germans were still making sporadic raids, not yet convinced that their own democracy could win out against the French king, but bent more upon food than glory. The brigade had marched into that town four hundred and twelve strong.

And now winter was here again, knocking with bony fingers upon their consciousness. Longingly they looked south and watched to see if the lieutenant gave any more heed to one direction than another.

Not for their lives would they have bothered him. Even Mawkey stayed afar. And it came to them with an unholy shock when they saw that a man had been passed through the sentries and was approaching the lieutenant with every evidence of accosting him. Several snatched at the fellow, but, imperiously, he swept on.

He might have been a ludicrous figure at a less tense moment. He was a powerful brute, his massive, hairy head set close down upon his oxlike shoulders. But about him he clutched some kind of cloak which would have heeled an ordinary being but only came to his thighs. On his head he had a cocked hat decorated with a plume. At his side swung a sword. On his chest was a gaudy ribbon fully two feet long.

Without ceremony he planted himself squarely before the lieutenant and lifted off his hat in a sweeping, grandiloquent bow.

The lieutenant was so astonished that he did not immediately return the salutation. Carefully he looked the fellow up and down, from heavy boots back again to the now-replaced cocked hat.

"General," began the intruder, "I come to pay my respects."

"I am no general, and if you wish to see me, get permission from my sergeant major. Pollard! Who let this by?"

"A moment," said the hairy one. "I have a proposition to offer you, one which will mean food and employment."

"You are very sure of yourself, fellow. Are we mercenaries that we can be bought?"

"Food is a matter of need, general. Allow me to introduce myself. I am Duke LeCroisaut."

"Duke? May I ask of what?"

"Of a town, general. I received the grant from the king not three years ago."

"King?"

"The King of France, His Majesty Renard the First. My credentials." And he took forth a scroll from his cloak and unwound it.

Without touching it, the lieutenant read the flowing phrases in the flourishing hand.

"Renard the First has been executed these last six months. And I, fellow, have nothing to do with the politics of France. We waste time, I think."

"General, do not judge so abruptly. My town, St. Hubert, has come into the hands of a brigand named Despard, a former private in the French army, who has seen fit to settle himself upon my people, oppressing them."

"This is nothing to me. Guard, escort this man beyond the sentries."

"But the food—" said the Duke with a leer.

The lieutenant shook his head at the guard, staying them for a moment. "What about this food?"

"The peasants have some. If you do as I ask, it shall be yours."

"Where is this town?"

"About a week's march south and west for you and your men; two days' march for myself."

"You evidently had *some* troops. What happened to them?"

"Perhaps unwisely, general, I dispensed with their services some months ago."

"Then you wish us to take a town, set you up and— Here! What's this?"

The fellow had sunk back against the concrete wall. He had been breathing with difficulty and his hand now sought his throat. His eyes began to protrude and some flecks of blood rose to his lips. He shook.

"An old wound—" he gasped. "Gas—"

The lieutenant unlimbered his pistol and slid off the catches.

"No! No, no!" screamed the Duke. "It is not soldier's sickness, I swear it! No! For the love of God, of your king—"

Smoke leaped from the lieutenant's hand and the roar of the shot rolled around the valley below. The empty tinkled on the stones. The lieutenant stepped away from the jerking body and made a sweeping motion with his arm.

"March in an hour. I do not have to caution you

to stay away from this body. Mawkey, pack my things."

"The guns?" said Gian, worriedly glancing at his pets and then beseechingly at the lieutenant.

"Detail men to haul them. They're light enough. But leave the three-inch. It would bog before the day was out."

"Si," said Gian gladly.

Shortly, Sergeant Hanley hurried up. "Third Regiment ready, sir."

An old man named Chipper piped, "First Regiment ready, sir."

Tou-tou bounded back and forth, making a final check from the muster roll he carried in his head. Then he snapped about and cried, "Second Regiment ready, sir."

Gian, overcome by new importance, saluted. "First Artillery ready, sir."

But it did not come off so well. The Fourth Brigade's First Artillery, a unit of .65-caliber field pieces, had been drowned to a man in a rising flood of the Somme while they strove to free their guns. For an instant the people here glanced around and knew how small they were, how many were dead and all that had gone before; they felt the chill in the wind which blew down from countless miles of graveyard.

"Weasel!" bawled the lieutenant. "Lead off at a thousand yards with your scouts. Bonchamp! Bring up the rear and shoot all stragglers. Chipper and

Herrero, wide out on the flanks! Fourth Brigade! *Forward!*"

The wind mourned along the deserted ridge, searching out something to twitch. But nearly all signs of the camp had been destroyed, just as there would be left no mark along the line of march by which another force could follow and attack. The wind had to content itself with the cloak of the dead man which it lifted off the legs time and again, and the gaudy ribbon which it rippled over the cooling face.

Malcolm matched the lieutenant's stride, glancing now and then at the man's quiet profile. Malcolm could not rid himself of the vision of the Duke trying to stop a bullet with his hands and screaming his pleas for life.

"Lieutenant," he said cautiously and respectfully, "if...if one of your men came down with soldier's sickness...would you shoot him like that?" Malcolm clearly meant himself.

The lieutenant did not glance at him. A shadow of distaste dropped over him and passed. "It has happened."

Malcolm avoided the finality of that statement. "But how would you know? How *do* you know that that fellow back there had it? Wouldn't gas—"

"Yes. It would."

"Then...then—"

"You've seen men die of soldier's sickness."

"Of course."

"You were in England when the first waves of it came. Over here, when one man got it, his squad got it shortly after. No one knows how it travels. Some say by lice, some by air. There was only one way to save a company and that was to execute the squad."

"But . . . but some are immune!"

"Maybe. The doctors who tried to make the tests died of it, also. Let's have an end of this, Malcolm."

They walked in silence for some time and gradually forgot about it. They had come to a broad valley matted with young trees. Here and there stone walls showed brokenly in the undergrowth; less frequently the gashed sides of a house stared forlornly with its gaping windows. A city had once flourished here. But the lieutenant's only interest in it was to see that the squirrels, rabbits and birds, those Geiger counters of the soldier, flourished through it with the ease of familiarity. It was not radioactive then. Nevertheless the rubble made the walking hard. And they clung to the outskirts, choosing rather an old battlefield than the tomb of the civilians. Pounded into the earth by rain of a dozen years lay an ancient tank, its gun silently covering the clouds which scurried south.

The men were not in any recognizable formation of march, but there was a plan of sorts despite the appearance of straggling. Loosely they formed a circle two hundred yards in diameter, a formation which would allow both a swift withdrawal into a compact defense unit from any angle of attack and would permit a swift enveloping of any obstacle met, the foremost point merely opening out and closing around. But the movements of the men themselves were quite independent of the organization, for they marched as the pilot of an ailing plane had once flown—not from field to field, but from cover to cover. All open spaces were either traversed at top speed, completely skirted, or else crawled through. The equidistant posts were very flexible of position according to the greatest danger of the terrain; these, too, were loose circles save for the rear guard, which was a long line, the better to pick up any willful stragglers or extricate any which had been trapped in the pits with which all this land abounded—pits which had the appearance of solid ground, built to impede troops and used now by peasants who found a need for clothing and equipment.

The one officer, if such he could be called, who had latitude of movement for his small group was Bulger. Bayonet thrust naked and ready in his belt, helmet pulled threateningly down over one eye, filthy warm flapping against his heels, he roved purposefully and thoroughly, rumbling from flank to flank and beyond, appearing magically inside and outside the circle of march. He would overrun the vanguard, inspect the ground ahead and then go rambling off with two or three scarecrows at his heels to poke into some suspicioned rise of ground and, sometimes, send a runner back to change the whole route of march to roll over the place and pick up cached supplies. After a good day Bulger would begin the evening meal by pulling birds, onions, old cans of beef from an unheard-of time, moldy loaves and wild potatoes from that warm which seemed to have the capacity of a full transport; for while the main discoveries had been shared around, Bulger took a joy in personal collection which outrivaled, if possible, his lieutenant's love of victory without casualty! These choice bits—and scarce enough they were—made up, first, the lieutenant's board and, second, the noncoms' fare. The brigade said of Bulger that he could hear a potato growing at the distance of four kilometers and could smell a can of beef at five.

The brigade flitted swiftly over an exposed chain of embankments which had been a railroad, long ago shelled out of existence and then robbed of its rails for bomb-proof beams. Bulger alone paused at the top, his hairy nostrils quivering avidly. He broke his trance and sped forward, presently lumbering past the vanguard. Weasel's narrow face popped alertly from beyond a bush.

"I don't hear anything," complained Weasel.

Bulger touched his nose pridefully and swept on, vanishing into the undergrowth ahead. As this was the mid portion of the valley, the only difference of level was a stream. This was revengefully eating away at an old mill dam, having already toppled the shell-bursted mill down the bank. But there was no ocular evidence whatever of anything unusual.

Telepathically quiet, the word skimmed through the brigade and the route of march shifted. Gian's artillery, which had been annoying its motive power by forbidding their taking the best cover, was balked by the stream until Gian, scurrying up and down the bank, found a shallow bar which had been built up by the downfall of an old bridge.

Bulger and his two scarecrows flickered beyond a screen of willows and vanished afield; one of the men, as runner, reappeared as a signpost and was scooped up by the advancing Weasel.

Presently the first sign of habitation was noted by the lieutenant. A rabbit snare flicked at his foot and sprang free. A moment later he brushed through a camouflage of small shrubs and was abruptly confronted by a plowed field. A crude arrangement consisting of a harness and a twisted stick had been turning back the furrows. A woman's cap lay on the untouched ground, but there was no other sign than this and tracks of those who had been there but a moment before.

Like a bear on the scent of a honey tree, Bulger was plunging along the fringe of wood, searching for a path and failing wholly to find it. The lieutenant, accompanied by Mawkey, came from cover and joined him.

"I smelled fresh earth," said Bulger, "and here it is. But where the seven devils is the trail?"

"There," said Mawkey, slightly disdainful. The tunnel looked as if it would refuse to admit anyone larger than a rat terrier, but Mawkey's eyes had seen a broken twig and so had been directed to this covered hole in the undergrowth.

"If they got energy enough to plow, they must have something to eat," reasoned Bulger with his usual single-mindedness. And immediately stooped to paw away the screen.

The lieutenant brought him back by a yank at his boot and, despite Bulger's size, landed him some ten feet from the hole. There was a sharp explosion and a crater appeared where the tunnel had been.

Bulger got to his knees looking sheepish.

"I'll be changing your diapers next," said the lieutenant to the assembled. "Falling for a planted grenade!" He faced about and signaled Weasel up with the vanguard. "Drop back with your kettles, Bulger, and be careful you don't drop one on your toe and kill yourself."

"Wait!" cried Bulger. "Please, sir. Wait! The wind's changed. I smell wood smoke!"

Weasel tested the air, mouth half-open, walking around in a small circle and looking skyward.

"There!" cried Bulger. "It's stronger now! Real dry wood burning." And, having redeemed himself, he rumbled after the scent, the slight Weasel trotting at his heels.

The lieutenant circled his right hand over his head, left hand extended palm down for caution. A few leaves stirred around the borders of the field. The brigade was moving up.

Presently one of Weasel's men bobbed out before the lieutenant. "Over to the right, sir."

The lieutenant swung in that direction and found Weasel and his vanguard standing around a pit, pulling up one of their number. The lieutenant gave a searching glance to the immediate surroundings and stepped forward. The trapped man's leg was bleeding where the stake at the bottom had gouged him. It was not serious and Mawkey laid the fellow out and bandaged it, having placed a chunk of spongy pitch in the wound.

There were some bones in the excavation, but no sign of any equipment. Alertly the lieutenant paced back and forth over the ground. In a moment he thrust a stick into a solid-appearing patch and so knocked the camouflage through. There were bones here as well.

"Pass the word," he said to a runner.

Bulger trundled his excited bulk back to them. "Sir, I've found it. About eighty houses and a dozen storerooms."

"Lead off."

The lieutenant strode along at Bulger's heels,

knocking in an occasional pit and warily avoiding the invitation of clear walkways, going through brush instead. The wood smoke was apparent to him now, though elusive.

They came to a flat expanse which was even more brush-covered than the surrounding terrain. There was nothing whatever to remark the presence of people and, had they come by earlier instead of at the time of the evening meal, it is certain they would have missed the village altogether.

The barest suggestion of heat waved in the air above the place. Only one wisp of smoke could be seen in the evening air, and the source of that could not immediately be traced. The lieutenant, from cover, examined the place minutely and it gradually began to take definite form for him.

He waited for some time, knowing that the brigade would envelop the place, and then turned to Mawkey. "I am going forward. Pick out and mark all the smoke spots and watch for my signal."

He pulled down his visor and drew his pistol. Then, wrapping his cloak tightly across his chest, he walked into the open! Instantly several shots snapped at him, two of them striking him and, for an instant, breaking his pace. Dark had been settling slowly for some little time, but the first indication he had of it was his ability to see the flashes from the rifles, which were orange in the half-light. Again shots drilled savagely around him. They came from the center in their highest concentration.

"Hello, the leader!" shouted the lieutenant in French.

The firing ceased and from nowhere in particular a voice rose from the flat earth. "We have no wish to see anyone! Go or we shall use grenades!"

"You are surrounded by the Fourth Brigade. We have artillery!"

There was a long pause and then, falsely aggressive, the same voice cried: "Devil take your artillery! We have much to answer!"

A grenade bounded from nowhere to the lieutenant's feet. It exploded with a bright flash. The lieutenant lifted himself from the depression some five yards beyond the place where it had gone off.

"One more chance. Surrender peaceably or take the consequences."

"Go to the devil!"

The lieutenant vanished into another patch of cover which was instantly raked by fire. He whistled shrilly twice. Instantly the villagers opened up at the borders of their field. But no shots came in return. Dusk was dropping swiftly now and it was that period of the day when it is both too dark and too light to see moving men.

The fire from the hidden emplacements slacked and stopped. Mystified and none too sure, the villagers conserved their scanty cartridges.

Short calls began to sound throughout the clearing, and the lieutenant waited until they had done. There was silence then for several minutes.

"We still offer you your chance to give over," stated the lieutenant. "All we require is billeting and food."

"We haven't changed our minds," said the leader.

"I shall count to ten. If you have not by that time, I cannot answer for the consequences." And he counted, very slowly, to ten. And there was no reply.

These people were tougher than the lieutenant had suspected. Usually his own careless appearance and the reports were sufficient to shake resolve. These survivors of all that science and politics could achieve had become survivor types of a rare order. He shrugged to himself. Little he cared.

He gave a short whistle in a certain key and there was a faint wave of movement through the clearing. Then, after a short time, the smoke began to clear from the air. Presently there sounded some coughs under the earth. And then more. The smoke which had vanished now began to thicken in the night. Throughout the village, handfuls of green leaves had been thrust down the camouflaged chimneys.

The coughing increased as the smoke increased, and there came wails of despair, the rattle of poles which sought to clear the obstructions, and the frenzied swearing of men trying to haul the green leaves from the grates.

The lieutenant lay upon his back and looked at the evening star, jewel-like in the darkening heavens. Other stars came slowly forth to make up constellations. A breeze played with the treetops and made them bow before the majesty of night.

"My general!" sobbed the leader. "We have seen the error of our decision. What mercy can we expect if we come up now?"

The lieutenant counted the stars in Cepheus and began upon the Little Bear.

"*My general!* For the love of Heaven, have mercy! There are children here! They are strangling! What can we expect if we come up now?"

With a sigh, the lieutenant gave his attention to the Great Bear and tried to make out the Swan, part of which was hidden by the drifting smoke.

There was a ripping of brush and the thump of a door thrown back and the clearing was immediately alight and fogged with billowing smoke. The lieutenant stood up. Soldiers materialized from the earth and people were herded into weeping, pleading groups. A few madmen gripped rifles, but were so obviously blinded that no one wasted ammunition upon them but merely wrenched the weapons away and pushed them into the crowds.

"Clear the chimneys," said the lieutenant. "Anyone who happens to have a mask, go below and clear the grates."

"I would never have surrendered," said the leader, groping toward the voice of command. "But

they were going out down there! For the love of
Heaven, don't kill us! We are friendly. Truly we are
friendly. We shall show you the storehouses, give
you beds, women, anything, but don't kill us!"

The lieutenant turned away from him in dis-
gust and watched his men dropping down steps into
the earth.

"We have so little but we give it all!" cried the
leader, pulling at the hem of the lieutenant's cape.
"But spare us!"

"Pollard," said the lieutenant, making a slight
motion with his hand. The leader was dragged away.

Presently Sergeants Chipper and Hanley drew
up before their commander. "I guess you can breathe
down there now, sir," said Hanley. "At least, on my
side. And I've taken a look at the inhabitants, sir,
havin' a little more time than some people. A
scrawny lot but there ain't a sick one among them."

"This half all cleared, sir," said the veteran
Chipper, indignant at this fancied gibe about his
age. "I made damn sure about the bugs. They still
must have insect powder, 'cause there ain't one." He
glared at Hanley.

"Pollard! Billet the men as the huts will take
them. Be certain to collect all weapons and mount
a guard upon them. Post sentries at fifty-yard intervals along the edge of the village."

"Yessir!" said Pollard.

Gian came up, sour because he had had no

chance to use his artillery. "Smoke," he muttered, disgustedly.

"Gian," said the lieutenant as though he had not overheard, "take a post to the north there on that little rise and hide your guns well. From there you can rake anything which puts in an appearance —with the exception, of course, of British troops, providing they are friendly. We'll depend upon you to give us a sound night's sleep."

Gian brightened and got two inches taller. "Anything, sir?"

"At your discretion."

"Yessssss, ssssssir!"

"Mawkey! Locate the leader's house and ask Toutou to please post a sentry over it."

Bulger dashed by, rubbing his hands together and swearing with delight as he uncovered storehouse after storehouse.

"Come along, Malcolm," said the lieutenant, presently.

They followed Mawkey down into the earth and found themselves in a large but low-ceilinged cavern. The roof was arched, supported by crudely hewn logs and railroad rails and smoothed off with a coating of dried white clay. The floor was carpeted with woven willows. Old fortress bunks were ranged along one wall and covered with army blankets. The furniture was all of branches, lashed with a kind of vine, with the exception of the table, which was topped by an old tank plate and supported artistically with upended one-pounders. The fireplace was of metal plate built into mud and stone and was fitted with several ingenious hinged shelves at variant heights above the grate. Evidently a fireplace was used because it smoked less than a stove. The utensils which hung about were all military, bearing various army stamps. Old blackout curtains were so arranged as to divide the place into sections, but they had strayed so far from their original purpose that they lacked two feet of reaching the roof.

Two other entrances led off, one near the bunks and another at the side of the outside door. Several pedestals were in place along the walls below roof cavities just big enough for a man's head; outside these were armored-car turrets projecting slightly into clumps of brush. The weapons had already been collected, but their racks occupied a prominent place. A series of channels edged the bottoms of the walls, made of bright airplane alloy, to catch any water which might come in from above.

The hut was more colorful than could be expected, for camouflage paint brightened the supporting columns and the bunks and table and several bunches of flowers were about, placed in vases hammered out of large shells.

The place was lit by an intricate system of polished metal plates which, in the daytime, brought the light down from the slots and, at night, scattered around the light from the fireplace.

The lieutenant grinned happily and stood up to the blaze to warm his hands. The sentry stepped into place at the bottom of the stairway and Mawkey closed and bolted the passageway doors.

Carstone looked in. "Any orders, sir?"

"Might post a couple of guns at the corner of the clearing to rake it in case."

"Yessir." He lingered for a moment.

"Yes?"

"I found another pneumatic tank, sir. They use it for water storage."

"Take it along."

"Thank you, sir."

"Ah," sighed the lieutenant happily, getting the weight of his cape from his shoulders. He unstrapped his helmet and gave it over to Mawkey.

"Near thing, sir," said Mawkey, poking a finger into the cape where a new slug had gone in exactly upon an old one.

"Mawkey, isn't there any way to get the bullets out of that thing? It weighs nine hundred pounds more every night I remove it."

"I saw some parachute silk on one of them women, sir. I could cut out the bullets and wad that stuff for a patch. It'd be safer, sir."

"By all means, Mawkey."

• • •

"Sir," said the sentry, "there's a bunch of people up here that want to see you."

The lieutenant made a motion with his hand and the sentry beckoned to someone up in the darkness. In a moment a woman, followed by two small children, came down. She looked as bravely as she could at the officers and then instinctively chose the lieutenant.

"You are our guest, sir," she said in halting English.

"Oh, yes, of course. You live here, eh? Well, there's plenty of room. By all means, bring your family down."

She looked relieved and made a beckoning motion to the top of the stairs. Three younger women and another child came down, followed by a very hesitant young man who stood defensively between two who were apparently his wives. A fifth woman came, helping a very aged dame whose eyes gleamed curiously as they inspected the officers. She, too, turned her attention to the lieutenant.

"You good gentlemen gave us a time," said the old woman in French.

"Hush," said one of the women, terrified at such boldness.

"Well, if they didn't kill us before, they aren't going to kill us now. Welcome, gentlemen. In payment for our lives these girls will get you a very good supper."

The five younger ones made haste to tuck the children into the far bunks, where they lay with their heads submerged and only their wide eyes showing. An attractive blonde hurried to the fire to replenish it and, so doing, dropped a stick of wood on the lieutenant's boot. She backed up, paralyzed.

"Don't mind Greta," said the old dame, sitting down and putting her toothless chin upon her cane. "She's a Belgian. Pierre here brought her back one day. You can't really blame a Belgian."

"Of course not," said the lieutenant. He looked curiously at the girl and smiled. Very cautiously she retrieved the piece of wood and cast it on the fire without again daring to look at him.

The young man had settled himself watchfully in the corner. His hands were enormous with toil; his eyes were brutish and sunken. He suggested an animal in the way his shoulders hunched. The girl Greta, sent for food from the locker at his side, walked clear of him, but he succeeded in seizing her wrist.

"You clumsy fool," he whispered harshly. "Do you want us all killed? I would not be surprised if you did that on purpose."

She wrenched away from him, her whole body suddenly like a flame. She struck him across the mouth and then yanked open the locker door in such a way that it pinned him in the corner while she got the mask container of flour.

The old woman was delighted at the young man's discomfiture. "Well! I have been wondering how she would answer you at last."

"Serves him right," whispered one of the women to another. "Picking up strays."

Their laughter stretched his intelligence beyond its elasticity and it snapped into rage. As soon as he was released he lunged at her and began to strike at her, roaring that she had pushed him away too long. But he stopped with a scream of pain and dropped to the floor, holding the side of his head. At a sign from the lieutenant, Mawkey had thrown his chains.

"I'll have no fighting here," said the lieutenant. "Throw him out."

The sentry's fingers fastened about the clod's collar and he was wrenched toward the door.

"Don't have him killed!" screamed the young man's wives, instantly down and clutching at the lieutenant's boots. One of the children began to howl in fright.

With distaste the lieutenant freed himself. Malcolm was grinning at the predicament. Greta stood with her straight back pressed hard against the wall, watching the lieutenant.

Pollard was down the steps in an instant with drawn automatic, knocking the young man out of the sentry's grip and down to the floor once more. The clod, snarling, rebounded. The room was full of flame and smoke and sound. The clod was down on his hands and knees, shaking his head like a groggy bull. He tried to reach Pollard and then, abruptly, the effort went out of him and he dropped to the mats, kicking straight out with his legs with lessening force. Pollard rolled him over with his toe. The arms flopped out and the blood-spattered remains of a face stonily regarded the beams above.

The two women who had protested started forward and then checked themselves, their eyes fixed upon the body. Slowly, then, they turned and went back to the bunks to quiet the wailing of the young one.

"Everything else all right?" said Pollard, smoothing his rumpled tunic.

"Carry on, sergeant," said the lieutenant, making a small upward motion with his hand.

Mawkey and the sentry towed the corpse up the steps. One of the women took a handful of reeds and hot water and cleansed the mat. Malcolm was gray.

The lieutenant warmed his hands before the blaze and the affair drifted out of his mind. Greta, eyes lowered, began to mix pancakes.

The business of supper went on and soon the lieutenant and Malcolm were eating at the table while Mawkey squatted over a pannikin in the corner. The sentry's back was expressive, moving restively and then springing erect in gladness as his fed relief came down to take over. The women sat at a smaller table by the fire with the exception of Greta, who waited with swift, quiet motions upon the officers and seemed to have forgotten about food. Angrily, at last, the old woman called to her and made her sit against the wall with her dinner.

"You are going far?" said the old woman.

"Far enough," said the lieutenant, smiling.

"You . . . you intend to carry away our stores?"

"We won't encumber ourselves with them, madame. An army fights badly upon a full stomach, contrary to an old belief."

She sighed her relief. "Then we will be able to live through the winter."

"Not unless you find some other way of disposing of your smoke," grinned the lieutenant.

"Ah, yes, that is true. But one does not always find an attack led by an officer of such talent."

"But, on the other hand, one sometimes does." The lieutenant stretched out his legs and leaned back comfortably, opening up his tunic collar and laying his pistol belt on the table with the flap open and the hilt toward him.

The old woman was about to speak again when the sentry snapped a challenge and then rolled aside on the steps to let Pollard come down.

Pollard, a fiend for duty, stood up censoriously, his long mustache sticking straight out.

"Well?" said the lieutenant.

"Sir, I have been checking Bulger's count on the storehouses. And—"

"Why count them? We're heading away from here at dawn."

Pollard received this without a blink. "I wanted to report, sir, that we have uncovered thirty-one soldiers."

"Feed them, shoot them or enlist them," said the lieutenant, "but let me digest a good dinner in peace."

"Sir, these men were naked in an underground cell. Fourteen of them are English. They have been used as plowhorses, sir. They say they were trapped and made slaves of, sir. One of them is balmy and I'm not sure of a couple more. They been cut up pretty bad with whips. Another says they're all that's left of the Sixty-third Lancers."

"Dixon! That's Dixon's regiment!" said Malcolm.

The lieutenant sat forward, interested. "Jolly Bill Dixon?"

"That's him," said Malcolm.

"They say he's dead, sir."

"By Heaven—" began Malcolm, starting up.

The lieutenant motioned him back into his chair. "Bring the leader of this village down here, Pollard."

"Yessir."

The old woman was thumping her cane nervously, her eyes fever-bright. "General—"

"Quiet," said Mawkey.

The room fell very still with only an occasional pop of the fire and the movement of shadows to give it life. The flame painted half the lieutenant's face, which was all the worse for having no particular expression beyond that of a man who has just enjoyed a full meal.

The leader was thrust down the steps in the hands of two guards. His small eyes were wild and bloodshot and he shook until no part of him was still. His sudden fright passed and he managed to fix his gaze on the lieutenant.

"When we came in," said the lieutenant, "I saw evidences of traps. There were bones in them and no equipment."

"The soldier's sickness! I swear, general—"

"And we have just located thirty-one prisoners. Soldiers you saw fit to convert into slaves."

"We have so much plowing, so few men—"

"You're guilty, then. Pollard, hand him over to those soldiers you found."

"No, no! Your excellency! They have not been mistreated, I swear it! We did not kill them even though they attempted to attack us—"

"When you take him out, parade him around a little so that this offal will know enough to respect a soldier," said the lieutenant.

"Your honor—"

"Carry on, Pollard."

"But your excellency! They'll tear me to pieces! They'll gouge out my eyes—"

"Am I to blame because you failed to treat them better?"

The old woman leaned toward the lieutenant. "My general, have mercy."

"Mercy?" said the lieutenant. "There's been none of that that I can remember where peasants and soldiers are concerned."

"But force will be met with force," said the old woman. "This is a good man. Must you rob this house of both its men in one night? What will we do for a leader? There are only seven hundred of us in this village and only a hundred and fifty of those are men—"

"If he is alive by morning, let him live. You have your orders, Pollard."

"I'll give them full rights!" wailed the leader. "A share in the fields, a voice in the council—"

"You might communicate that to those fellows," said the lieutenant to Pollard. "No man is good for a soldier if he allows himself to be trapped in the first place. Carry on."

The leader was led away and the lieutenant relaxed again. Greta filled his dixie with wine and he sipped at it.

The other women in the room were very still. The children did not cry now. The fire died slowly down.

Shortly there was a commotion at the top of the steps and the sentry lounging there reared up with his rifle crossed, barring passage to several men who seemed to desire, above all things, to dash down and worship the officer who had set them free. Finally understanding that the guard would have none of them, they went away.

"—a voice in council," the leader was saying, falsely hearty. "For some time I've kept my eye on you— Glad to have such an addition—"

The women in the room started breathing again. A child whimpered and was caressed to sleep. Wood was tossed upon the fire and the room became cheerfully light.

"You are a good man, my general," said the old woman in a husky voice.

Greta sat in the recess of the chimney seat, her lovely body perfectly still, her eyes steady upon the lieutenant.

A long time after, the lieutenant lay in the bunk farthest from the door, gazing at the dying coals upon the grate, pleasantly aware of a suspension in time. Tomorrow they would again be on the march, heading back to G.H.Q. and an uncertain finish. He was quite aware, for the first time, that the war was done. He was aware, too, with ever so little sadness, that England and his people were barred to him, had rejected him, perhaps forever.

The fire died lower and most of the people of the household slept, the women in the tiers of bunks near the steps, the children with them. Malcolm was rolled in a blanket by the fire. At the far end of the dwelling in a wide bed which had been shaken and dusted well the lieutenant watched the fire dying. He watched through a slit in the curtains which masked him from the remainder of the room.

He was unconsciously aware of Mawkey lying just behind the slit as an active, living barrier to anything which might seek to approach his invaluable and beloved commander. There was a rustle of parachute silk and the creak of a bunk in the forward partition of the room. And the lieutenant was suddenly alert, but not to danger. Naked feet fell uncertainly amongst the reeds. The fire threw the curves of a shadow softly on the curtain. The footsteps came nearer.

As the snake strikes, Mawkey fastened savagely on her ankle as she would have crossed to the lieutenant. It was Greta.

The lieutenant raised on his elbow and whispered hoarsely, "Let her go, you fool!"

Mawkey came to himself. Her skin was soft under his hand and her fingers held no weapon. In the soft firelight the parachute silk revealed the rondeur of a lovely body. Mawkey shamefacedly withdrew his hands. And when again she had her courage up she stepped over him and went on toward the large bed in the deepest recess of the room.

Mawkey drew the curtains shut as he rolled outside them. For a little he listened to the whispers, then at last, the girl's soft rich laugh. He smiled, pleased.

One by one the glowing coals went out. Mawkey slept.

Chapter IV

Through the morning, the brigade mounted ridge after ridge, keeping to no definite course but working toward a certain objective by arcs and angles. It was hot work and, to Malcolm, senseless, for they only succeeded in exposing themselves to several random shots by hopeful snipers in high rocks who vanished like their powder smoke upon approach—wanderers who coveted a knapsack or two, could they drop it into a ravine and beyond the immediate concern of the troops.

It had taken Malcolm only forty-eight hours of fast traveling to get from the G.H.Q. to the Fourth Brigade, and it was taking the lieutenant interminable days of circuitous march to make the return. Malcolm had followed the high ground with a relief map. It would be very different when *he* had this command, he thought.

Malcolm's crossness was not lost upon the lieutenant, but it did not wear upon him until they halted wearily at noon on a hill which commanded all approaches.

"What's the matter?" said the lieutenant.

Malcolm looked at him innocently. "Nothing."

"Come on, have it out."

"Well— I think you should have had that village leader shot. Dixon was our friend."

The lieutenant knew that this was a dodge, but he answered. "We had no evidence that those people killed Dixon. Jolly Bill was entirely too good an officer to be rolled down by peasants."

"I never knew you needed evidence to execute a man."

"To put you straight on the matter, I did execute him. Now, are you satisfied?"

"How's this? Why, I saw him with my own eyes bidding us good-bye."

"And you saw Tou-tou issuing their rifles to the thirty-one Pollard dug out of the ground. Tell me, Malcolm, why should I thicken up the atmosphere of that hut any further and so annoy myself when the task was clearly finished at the release of the prisoners? Peasants do strange things. While we were there, there might have been an incident of some sort if the leader had been killed. It is done, anyway."

"You mean those soldiers—"

"Of course. The village, you might say, has passed under a military regime. And why not? There were few enough men there when we arrived. They should appreciate the additional thirty-one. And who knows but what the place may become all the stronger therefor? However, such matters are outside my domain."

Malcolm was not mollified in the least. He gazed very uneasily at the lieutenant, suddenly unsure in the presence of such cold thoroughness. In fact, he began to feel sorry for the leader, forgetting completely that he had trapped soldiers and enslaved them.

"Sometimes I don't understand you," said Malcolm. "Maybe it is because I have been less long at the front than you. Maybe I'm just a staff officer and always will be. But— Well, you're not consistent. You were courteous to the Russian commander and yet you treated that village leader like a cur."

The lieutenant had not thought about it. Mawkey came up and spread lunch out on a rock and the two officers ate silently for some time. The lieutenant finished and sat back, looking down across the autumn-colored valley without really seeing it.

At last, he spoke. "I suppose it was because I felt that way. Maybe there are so few of the officers' corps left that we have a feeling we ought to preserve ourselves. Maybe it's because all officers have been taught the necessity of exalting their rank and being as above that of the civilians. Civilians started all this mess anyway, didn't they? Bungling statesmanship, trade mongering, their 'let the soldier do the dirty work' philosophy, these things started it. The Russian was a fellow craftsman. But the leader of that village commune— Bah! A stupid blunderer, raised up from filth by guile, a peasant without polish or courage— The thought revolts me." He was silent for a while, staring out at the painted slopes. And then: "There are so few of us left."

Malcolm, a little awed now by the quiet sadness he had drawn forth, could not venture to carry it forward. He had been dwelling, in the main, upon this circuitous marching and had not quite the courage to speak boldly in criticism of a commander in the field.

All that afternoon they stole wraithlike through the wilderness, beating up only rabbits and birds. But by night they had come into a one-time industrial area which scarred the earth for a mile around with the fragments of buildings and machinery.

Although this city had been splattered into atoms at the very beginning of the war, it had been rebuilt, in lessening degree, in each lull which followed in order to utilize the coal here found. But after each retreating army had damaged the mines turn after ceaseless turn, at last they were wholly unworkable.

Water tanks leaned crazily—great blobs of rust

against the sky. Buildings were heaps of rubble, overgrown with creeping vines and brown weeds. Within a few years the place would be swallowed except for the few battered walls which made ragged patterns against the hazy dusk. Fused glass crunched under foot and twisted chunks of metal attested the violence of thermite bombs and shells.

The brigade, having ascertained that the place was not radioactive, filtered through the tangle, alert and silent. Gian's men sweated the light guns over the unevenness, cursing both guns and the laborious works of man.

The lieutenant caught sight of the Weasel's runner signaling him ahead from the side of an overturned railroad car. He quickened his pace and followed the fellow up to the vanguard.

Weasel, his small self very still, pointed mutely to a crazily suspended railroad rail which jutted out from a wall like a gibbet. It was a gibbet.

Four soldiers, their necks drawn to twice their length, were rotting in their uniforms, swaying to and fro in the gentle wind. Below them was a painted scrawl upon the stone:

SOLDIERS! MOVE ON!

"British," whispered Pollard, coming up.

The lieutenant looked around. Ahead he could see the mine entrances and piles of waste which bore lines like trails. He gave the place a careful scout and returned to his men.

"I hear people down there," said Weasel, ear to earth.

A bullet smashed into the truck of a railroad car and went yowling away like a broken banjo string.

"I think," said the lieutenant, "that this is a very good place to spend the night. *Gian! Guns front into action!*"

All the following day and the day after, Malcolm was increasingly morose. He had encountered a problem which he could not solve and it was giving him nerves. He had known the lieutenant very casually at Sandhurst when they were sixteen and cadets. But he did not remember such a man as this, rather, a somewhat quiet, cheerful lad with only a hint of the devil in his eyes. But the blank had been filled by seven battlesome years, two for the lieutenant in England, five for Malcolm. And the five which the lieutenant had spent on the Continent seemed to have forged a steel blade which might stab anywhere.

It was all so irrational! Malcolm had counted on his order and the habit of obedience to the source to bring the lieutenant back. That and tales about what Victor wished to do for the lieutenant. But the lieutenant's mind was not one to run in grooves or to be duped, and here he was, walking back to a loss of command! And Malcolm was fairly certain now that the lieutenant *knew* what was waiting for him. Hadn't the lieutenant failed to take any cognizance of the general orders to reorganize on the outline of the B.C.P.? Hadn't he been all too successful in his campaigning—too successful to be safe? Certainly such a man, asserting such independence, could not be left with a body of troops while the general staff was so weak.

And Malcolm was suffering from jealousy. He was used to a close understanding between an officer and his troops, yes, but these fellows actually seemed to wriggle when the lieutenant saw fit to look at them. It was rather disgusting. Well, that would be changed. They'd recognize their rights, these fellows, and know that the new order of things was best. A clever officer was better off under a committee than he was by himself, for he could always manipulate the membership of that committee with benefit to himself and could always blame all failure upon it. Soldiers were such stupid brutes.

Malcolm could understand that the lieutenant was not anxious to check in at G.H.Q., in the light of what he must know. But why, then, didn't he just quietly put a bullet in Malcolm and head south, forgetting that any organization such as G.H.Q. ever existed?

This devious traveling was an annoyance to a man who feels he is constantly being put off from control of his command. And Malcolm had thought about it so often and so long that he was now under the impression that he was truly commanding here and so every order from the lieutenant came as a definite affront.

Then, damn it, those people in that first village had instinctively turned to the lieutenant! And the people there at the mines, even though they had been terribly knocked about in the short fight, had calmed into quiet obedience as soon as the lieutenant confronted them with his orders.

And last night, when they had raided that old fort, the noncom in charge had almost licked the lieutenant's boots!

This brigade was all wrong. Their haversacks were stuffed. Forty impressed carriers were lugging the guns and the carts of provisions. It was glutting itself from the best in the countryside, poor as that best was, but it was also marching and fighting like people possessed. What was the sense of that when a two-day fast march would take them across the looted soil which stood like a band around G.H.Q.? What use did the lieutenant have for all this loot?

That night, secure in a cave-pocked hill which had been taken by assault with the loss of only one man and that a carrier, Malcolm brooded long. He felt he had a very definite quarrel with the lieutenant and, the way Malcolm stood with Victor, a quarrel which would very soon be settled.

The G.H.Q. of the B.E.F. in France was the only thing of permanence which had survived the last mass bombardments. It had been constructed under the direct supervision of the general staff some fifteen years before and was, therefore, probably the only safe refuge in this, now borderless, country. Every artifice discovered for camouflaging and armor-plating a fortress had gone into its making, until neither shell nor gas could make the slightest impression upon it. And its deepest recesses were even proof against atom bombs and radioactive dust. Sickness and bacteria only took toll of men.

Spreading some fifty thousand square yards under the earth, it occupied the better part of a rocky hill. No chamber in it was less shallow than eighty feet and all chambers were designed to withstand, at a blow, the combined blasts of twenty town busters. The appointment had overlooked nothing by way of safety and so the G.H.Q. had remained stationary, quite some distance from the wreck of Paris and still far enough from the sea to prohibit attack from that quarter. The thirty-nine generals who had, in turn, commanded here had only lacked provision for the prevention of casualty through politics.

Every ventilator was a fortress in itself, guarded by an intricate maze of filters which took all impurity from the air. In addition to this, each chamber contained oxygen tanks sufficient for a hundred men for one month. Water was plentiful, for the place was served by half a dozen artesian wells, two of which operated on their own pressure. The lighting was alcohol driven with a helio-mirror system as auxiliary. The communications alone had been neglected, for provision had been made for telephones and radio only, whereas the lines of the former had long gone dangling for want of copper and the latter had been useless when storage batteries for field receivers had gradually become exhausted, never to be replaced. Radio communication was occasionally established even yet with England, but the occasion for this had now vanished.

Outwardly the place was just a hill, the countryside about rather torn up by constant shelling and bombing and the approach too open to be attempted. There were a dozen such rises in the neighborhood and many an enemy pilot had mistaken one for the other until the whole terrain was similarly marked. The rusty wrecks of charred tanks and crumpled planes gradually merged with the mud.

In short, the place was an ideal G.H.Q. The generals, in perfect safety, could send the army out to die.

When the lieutenant had last seen it, it had been summer. But the effect of gas upon undergrowth was enough to make little difference between summer and late autumn.

A drizzle of rain was turning the flats into bogs and obscuring the horizon and the brigade marched with helmet visors down and collars up, more because it was habit than because their thin clothing could keep out the wet. They had only had a morning of this but still they were all of a color, and that was of mud.

But there were no complaints to be heard, for the rains had held off much longer than usual this fall, and because an outfit whose bellies are full would not feel right unless something bad came along with the good.

At one time, out this far, there had been photo-electric sentries and land mines, but as these had worn out and had been exploded by occasional attacks, they had not been replaced. In fact, the brigade was almost upon the hill itself before they were decried.

"Soldiers," sniffed Weasel to Bulger in derision. "We could have walked in and stole their socks if we'd been trying."

"They get that way," said Bulger. "That was always the trouble with forts. Eight years ago I said it always happened. They feel so safe they don't even bother to watch. You give a soldier a full belly and some sandbags to dig into and he goes to sleep."

"Naw, he don't," said Weasel. "He sits around and thinks, and pretty soon he's got it figured out that he's a Communist or a Socialist or an Individualist, and the next thing you know he shoots the officers and changes the government. I says we'd still have a king in England if they hadn't had bases to bore the soldiers to death. It ain't fightin' that ruins governments. It's eatin'."

"There ain't nothin' wrong with eatin'," said Bulger, defensively.

"Not when there's fightin'. All eat and no fight makes Tommy a politician."

"They ain't doin' much eatin' around here," said Bulger, having come within surveyal distance of the first sentry.

Indeed, the man was very gaunt. His buckle was fastened around his spine and his cheeks showed the outline of his teeth. There was a dreary hopelessness about him, and when he was supposed to port his arms he lifted the rifle up an inch or two to show that he knew he should and let the lieutenant through without so much as whispering to turn out the guard.

The Fourth Brigade went down the incline into the earth, gun wheels rumbling up the echoes. They paused in the first chamber until an officer came out of the guardroom.

"Fourth Brigade?"

"Right," said the lieutenant.

"I am Major Sterling. Oh! Hello, Malcolm. By George, old chap, we wondered what on earth had happened to you."

"We took a personally conducted tour of Europe," said Malcolm, for the first time feeling at ease when in the lieutenant's presence, and therefore giving vent to what he really thought.

"Well, now. We waited. Couldn't see what had happened. But you're here, and that's what matters. Malcolm, if I were you, I'd quarter my men in the north section. We've got sixteen hundred here, all told, and you make almost eighteen hundred. Most everyone is quartered in the north section in those old thousand-man barracks. It's quite light and roomy now and it's better that everybody is together."

The lieutenant was not particularly surprised that the major should call them Malcolm's troops; he was only annoyed by the actual fact. They were not Malcolm's yet.

"Sergeant major Pollard," said the lieutenant. "You will quarter the brigade in the north section. I shall be in to make an inspection as soon as I have paid my respects to General Victor."

"Yessir," said Pollard. "And the carriers, sir?"

"Retain them until further orders. I daresay they're happy enough."

"Yessir." He hesitated, and then saluted and turned away. He had not quite dared wish the lieutenant luck, no matter how much he wanted to do so.

The lieutenant looked at Sterling. He did not like the fellow. General Victor had brought rabble with him instead of a staff. Every bootlicker that had skulked throughout the war in the shelters of London had been ousted by the last reversal of government. Sending a man to France since the quarantine was placed was tantamount to exiling him for life. None of these fellows had seen real war. They had dodged bombs and fawned upon superiors. In the latter they had become very adept.

Long ago, the last competent officer had taken

the field. And now, where were they? Adrift somewhere in Europe or deposed and languishing here without command.

Major Sterling was not quite able to bear the censure which was leveled upon him by the lieutenant's eyes, nor did he like the slight smile which lingered about the mouth. There were around eighty-seven field officers still unreported and it was apparent now that they would never report; why, then, should a man with a record as brilliant as the lieutenant's come back? Only twenty-one fragments of organizations had come in, and these because of starvation. But the Fourth Brigade, quite obviously, was not starving. However, it was a strange thing, this habit of duty.

"This orderly will show you your quarters," said Major Sterling. "You will please prepare a written report and send it, by him, to the adjutant colonel."

Dismissed, the lieutenant looked for a moment at Malcolm who, very obviously, was on his way right now to see General Victor. Malcolm, too, was unable to support the directness of those eyes. The lieutenant followed the orderly and Mawkey followed the lieutenant.

They went deeper into the labyrinth, along dank corridors which long had gone unswept and unlit. Here and there the concrete had faulted and drips of water were outlined by a pattern of moss.

Row upon row of officers' apartments were musty with disuse, their doors, untouched for two years and more, sagging out from their weary hinges. The lieutenant remembered this place from its yesterdays. Five years before, when England had sent her last flood of men to the Continent and when the army here was still great and proud, these corridors had resounded with cheerful voices and hurrying boots; sergeant majors had bustled along to receive or to obey orders; subalterns' dog-robbers worried themselves frantic as they raced about with hot water and laundry; canteen runners had flashed along with their trays of drinks; and officers would have popped forth as the word raced along to give him greeting and beg for news.

It was all quiet now. Not even a rat scuttled in the dead gloom. These voices which should have called out a welcome were forever stilled, these faces were decomposed in some common grave out in the endless leagues of mud. Only the ghosts were here, crying a little, naked and cold and forgotten—or was it just the wind?

The runner tiredly indicated a door and slumped down on the bench outside as though the effort had been too much. Mawkey entered and finally found the trap which opened the helio-mirror.

The apartment was littered with scraps of baggage, Gladstones and locker trunks and valises. It had been a long while since they had been ransacked for valuables and the mold was thick and clammy upon them. Useless knicks, dear only to their dead owners, were thrown carelessly about. A large picture of a girl lay in the center of the room. A careless foot had broken the glass and the dampness had seeped in to almost blot the face with dirt. A sheaf of letters were scattered about, crumpled and smudged; one on the table was decipherable only as far as "My dearest Tim. I know this will find you safe and—" A pair of boots, too well-tailored to be comfortable, stuck out from the lid of a locker. But the rats had eaten the leather nearly to the soles.

The lieutenant leaned against the table while Mawkey tried to straighten the place by heaving everything into a trunk. The lieutenant's eyes wandered up and fastened upon a stenciled box, the last piece of baggage upon the rack, where all of it had been placed so carefully so long ago.

Forsythe, A. J.
Col. Cmmdg. 4th Brigade, 2nd Div.
10th Army Corps
B.E.F.

For an instant there flashed across the lieutenant's memory the picture of a straight-backed, gray-mustached soldier, trying hard not to show the agony of his wound as he looked levelly at the lieutenant.

"They're gone, son. They're gone and I'm gone. It is up to you now, son."

• • •

Suddenly the lieutenant was filled with a great restlessness. Angrily, he swept the litter from the table and began to pace back and forth from wall to wall. Mawkey was startled, for he had never seen his lieutenant give way to any emotion before which even slightly resembled nerves. Hastily the hunchback finished cramming the refuse into the trunk and got the baggage out of the way. He set the lieutenant's effects upon a bunk and got out the razor and some clean clothing and started away to see if he could find any hot water.

"I'm not changing," said the lieutenant.

Mawkey looked at the mud-caked cape and the crusted boots and then turned back to put away the clean clothes.

"Get me some paper."

Mawkey found some in the refuse and smoothed it out upon the table. He put a pencil down and pulled up a chair.

The lieutenant sat and wrote.

Report 4th Brigade May to Nov. 1
To General Commanding B.E.F.
From Lieutenant Commanding 4th Brigade
Via Adjutant Colonel, official channels

1. The 4th Brigade patrolled region north of Amiens.
2. The 4th Brigade met and defeated several commands of enemy troops.

3. The 4th Brigade provisioned itself on the country.
4. The 4th Brigade now numbers 168 men, 5 senior noncoms, 1 officer.
5. The 4th Brigade, on receiving orders, reported to G.H.Q.

> Commanding Officer
> 4th Brigade

Mawkey gave the report to the runner, who slouched off with it trailing limply from his fingers.

"Beg pardon, sir," said Mawkey.

"Well?"

"I don't like this, sir."

The lieutenant looked at him.

"That Captain Malcolm, sir. He is thought pretty well of here, I think. He is a staff officer. One of them thoroughgoing politicians, beggin' your pardon, sir."

"Well?"

"I am pretty sure that everybody is getting ready to leave this place. The men looked starved and there ain't anything in the country around here. I think that is why we were called back. Beggin' the lieutenant's pardon."

"And what of that?"

"I think Captain Malcolm is going to be given command of the brigade, sir. He acted like that and he ain't any field officer. He's weak and he's soft and all he knows how to do—"

"You are speaking of an officer, Mawkey."

"Beg pardon, sir. But I'm speakin' of one of them staff things that come over a couple years ago. And the B.C.P. was always so rotten that whatever they wanted to get rid of must've been pretty—"

"Mawkey!"

"Yessir."

Mawkey withdrew and began to fuss with the forgotten baggage, seeing if there was anything there that his lieutenant could use. Now and then he bent a glance at his officer. Plainly he was worried.

In two hours the runner dragged himself up to the door to announce that the lieutenant was ordered to report to the adjutant colonel and the officer followed him.

As they passed the batman by the door, Mawkey whispered: "Be careful, sir."

They went down, down, down into the earth until it seemed that the staff of G.H.Q. wanted to be as close as possible to the devil. The lieutenant noted the emptiness and filth of the fortress in general and was inclined to agree with Mawkey that the place would soon be abandoned.

They came at last to the office of the adjutant colonel, a place wholly encased in lead plate so that voices repeated themselves hollowly and endlessly. This room did not bear the same stamp as the rest of the fortress. The five juniors who sat at desks in the outer chamber did not appear to be starved. Their uniforms were strictly regulation and, if a little old, were not much worn; they had had, after all, the whole fortress to pick from. There was something unhealthy about these fellows which the lieutenant could not immediately recognize. He was used to men tanned by wind and sun and darkened with dirt, men who had hard faces and wasted few words or actions. These faces were like women's, and not very reputable women at that. They seemed to be somewhat amused by the lieutenant's appearance and, as soon as he had passed, went back to their ceaseless chattering.

The adjutant colonel's name was Graves and certainly he resembled nothing more than an undertaker. He sat at his desk as though it was a coffin and he was melancholy about the dear, dead deceased. He was a dark, small, greasy man and his eyes were not honestly evil like Mawkey's; they were masked and hypocritical.

Graves showed scant attention to the lieutenant, but required him to stand for some minutes in front of the desk before he saw fit to glance up. Then he did not speak, but sent a junior in to find if the lieutenant could be seen.

The junior came back and Graves stood up. Graves went down the hall and stepped into a larger office encased in even thicker lead plate.

"Officer commanding the Fourth Brigade, Second Division, Tenth Army Corps," said Graves. He beckoned the lieutenant to follow him in. Another junior announced them in the inner chamber and then the lieutenant was beckoned into a large room.

A table occupied most of the space and about the table sat men much like those in the adjutant's outer office. They were all shaven and brushed and anointed and wore their insignia conspicuously. They wanted no mistake made about their rank, which was high, or their staff position, which they thought was high.

The lieutenant was sensible of their regard and knew they were staring somewhat dismayed at the mud which caked the battle cloak and the boots and the dirt which stained the unshaven face. It did not come to them immediately that the lieutenant's hands were covered by the cape and that the cape was bullet proof. It was very unseemly that he should come so armed, and censure was directed at the adjutant, all in silence.

General Victor, a very small and dehydrated man with too large a head and too small a mouth, sat at the head of the table. He glanced once at the lieutenant and then, finding that the eyes had a shocking power, hastily returned to a perusal of reports. He did not much like these field officers. They came in smelling of battle and full of comment upon their orders and generally made a man feel unsure of himself.

The lieutenant thought that this looked more like a court-martial than a conference. He caught sight of Malcolm, now beautifully groomed, standing against the wall, looking carefully disinterested.

A colonel named Smythe, on Victor's right, glanced to Victor for permission and then, receiving it, turned to the lieutenant. In Smythe's hand was the lieutenant's report.

"This is very little to submit," said Smythe.

"It is complete enough," said the lieutenant.

"But you give no detail of casualties or desertions or troops fought."

"I knew you wouldn't be interested," said the lieutenant.

New interest came into the eyes about the table, for the lieutenant's tone was not in the least tempered with courtesy.

"Come now," said Smythe, "give us an account. We must know what troops there are out there which might impede our movements."

"There are about a thousand Russians heading south to Italy. They are the last of the Imperial White Russian Army. You might possibly contact them, but I doubt it."

"That's better," said Smythe, with a toothy smile which made him look very much like a rabbit. "Now, we have had reports about roving bands of soldiers, without officers, who have been laying waste the countryside. Have you met some of these?"

"Why should I?"

"Why should you? My dear fellow, it is the duty—"

"I was ordered to return here. I think the

countryside will take care of those who still remain of the enemy—and of our own troops, too."

"We did not request an opinion," said Smythe.

"But you have it," said the lieutenant. He had been taking accurate stock of the room and had found that four enlisted men were posted at the board and two others stood behind Victor.

"What are those fellows doing here?" said the lieutenant, with a motion in their general direction.

"The Soldiers' Council representatives," said Smythe. And then, with sarcasm: "Of course, if you object—" The titter about the board pleased him.

The representatives were witless-looking fellows, rather better fed than their compatriots of the barracks. They did not instantly perceive that they had been affronted, and when they did it was too late.

"We have a report here," said Smythe, "that you failed to organize, at any time, or permit the organization of a soldiers' council in your brigade. Is that true?"

"Yes."

"And I believe, according to the record here, that we sent out a man named Farquarson, a private, to help organize such a council in your brigade. He does not seem to be with you now and we can get no word of him from your troops."

"He was killed," said the lieutenant.

"What's this?"

"If you'd sent a soldier he might have lived a

while. But as it was, the first time we were under fire he was shot."

"You infer that you—"

"I infer nothing, gentlemen. It was not necessary to shoot the troublemaker myself. It takes a man to live these days." And he looked around the board, plainly not finding any.

Smythe and the general put their heads together and whispered, glancing at the lieutenant the while. Then Victor whispered something to the officer on his left, who whispered to the next, and so on about the board. At last Smythe had it back again and whispered to the two soldiers back of the general, who both nodded stupidly.

Squaring himself about, Smythe addressed the lieutenant. "We have come to the conclusion that you are incompetent in the direction of your command, sir. We have decided that you shall be removed from that office. Because you have not sufficient rank to be attached to the staff, you will consider yourself as a supernumerary to the garrison without duties and, consequently, on half rations."

"And my command?" said the lieutenant.

"Will be provided for carefully. I believe Captain Malcolm here is better fitted for the duty. The Fourth Brigade will be assimilated as a company by the First Brigade of the First Division of the First Army Corps and will be stricken from the Army

List. You will please turn over to Captain Malcolm your records and standards."

"Gentlemen," said the lieutenant, "your wishes are law. May I ask one question?"

"Certainly," said Smythe, somewhat mollified by this statement, which he took to be complete acquiescence.

"You intend to leave this place. I can perhaps give you some data upon the conditions in the surrounding countryside, where you can get provisions and so on."

"I am afraid we do not need your advice," said Smythe "But there is no reason not to tell you that we intend to take a certain area far to the south which is reported to be fertile. And, by the way, lieutenant, I do not believe there is any occasion for you to revisit your own troops. The guard will be informed to include your name on the list of those barred from communicating with the men. There are several of your field officers here, and we can't have any trouble, you know."

"I am barred—"

"Certainly. It is necessity. Colonel Graves, will you please make certain that even his batman is sent to the barrack before the lieutenant returns to his quarters."

"This, then," said the lieutenant, "is arrest!"

Smythe shrugged. "That is a hard name. You do not seem to share our political views and as such your opinions must, of course, be isolated. Your room probably should be changed as well."

"Does it come to you that you gentlemen may regret this?"

"Come, come," said Smythe, amused. "No threats, now. You are excused, lieutenant."

Captain Malcolm could not help smiling over his complete victory.

Name: _____

Address: _____

City: _____ State: ____ Zip: _____

Chapter V

The lieutenant discovered his quarters moved to the south passages, at the greatest possible distance from his troops. Of Mawkey there was no sign; only the pack on the table showed that he had been there.

When the orderly had shuffled away, the lieutenant unfastened his cloak from about his shoulders and dropped it to the table. He put his helmet upon it but he did not remove his side arms. It had rather amused him that nobody had quite dared ask for his weapons, but now even that faded. Dispiritedly he sat down on a stool and began to clean the mud from his boots with a splinter from the table.

That he was preoccupied completely showed when it became apparent that he was not alone in the room. The oversight, when he noted it, alarmed him for it indicated how the grip on himself had slipped. This would never do. An officer with nerves was a dead officer.

A large, hopeless-looking youth swung his legs down from an upper bunk. He seemed to have lost all pride in both self and appearance for his blond hair was matted and snarled and his greasy tunic was buttoned awry where it was buttoned at all. His dull insignia showed that he was a subaltern. He looked disinterestedly at the lieutenant.

From the bunk opposite another pair of legs showed and the lieutenant glanced in that direction. This second officer was a major, probably in his thirties, though his hair was already gray. He, too, was a big man, bearing that stamp of hopelessness which characterized the first. A black patch covered the place where his left eye had been and his left sleeve was tucked into his belt. But he still took care of his person, for his mustache was carefully trimmed and his jowl blue with the razor. His right eye brightened.

"May I introduce myself?" he said. "I am Major Swinburne and that lad there is Mr. Carstair, an Australian."

"Pleased," said the lieutenant, going back to work on his boots.

"What organization?" asked Major Swinburne.

"Fourth Brigade, Second Division, Tenth Army Corps, commanding."

"Well, well! You still have your organization, then. My regiment has been stricken from the Army

List and Mr. Carstair's company as well. I say, old boy, if you don't mind my being curious, just how did you manage to keep your command away from those ghouls?"

"Until I am notified in writing and until my color bearer gives up our standard, the Fourth Brigade still exists and I am still in command."

A monotonous kind of laughter issued for several seconds from the subaltern's throat and then, while he still went through the expression, ceased to make any sound.

"Quite amusing, no doubt," said the lieutenant.

"Don't be hard on the lad," said the major. "He came out four years ago and he's seen every officer of his regiment killed. He brought in his company nearly a year ago and he has not been out of this fortress since, nor has he had duty."

"And you?"

"I've only been here a month," said Swinburne, "but it is pretty clear to me now that all field officers are being eliminated from their commands and that General Victor and that crackpot Smythe are thinking of setting up some sort of dukedom or some such thing. I came in just before all communication was cut off with London and so I got caught."

"I understood," said the lieutenant, "that twenty-one commands have reported in. Am I to presume that the rest of the officers are being similarly treated?"

"They were," said Swinburne.

"And where are they?"

"There are still thirty or forty organizations out so far as I know. All but Carstair and myself have managed to get out of here and join them, one way or another."

"And you are telling me that field officers deserted their outfits here?"

"Not exactly. There were desertions of noncoms and a few men as well."

"Then the place has nothing but staff officers and very few field noncoms?"

"Yes."

The lieutenant smiled.

"I fail," said Major Swinburne, "to see anything funny in that."

"The confidence of these Tommy-come-afters astounds me," said the lieutenant. "That is all."

"They have little to fear," said Major Swinburne. "Before they left England they were vaccinated against soldier's sickness."

"What's this? There is a vaccine?"

"It was produced in very small quantities by culturing human blood. I understand that only the governmental heads and the staffs have been given it."

"Our natural immunity to it is low enough, Heaven knows," said the lieutenant. "Well! So they can thumb their tails at soldier's sickness. No wonder they're still alive." And again he laughed quietly.

"You seem to be easily amused," said Carstair resentfully.

"I was thinking of those poor little weaklings walking through the mud out there, not getting their tea on time and being knocked off left and right by every sniper that comes along. The joke of it is, they've been moles so long they think war and disease cleaned the country. Why, a subaltern with twenty men could outmaneuver them and annihilate them before breakfast."

"Not so easily. Some of them have been on field service in central Germany," said Major Swinburne. "Do not underrate them. As I see it, they intend to take over this entire district, only going south to get into a region where there is food. Most of the still-extant organizations, you see, have headed for the Balkans and the Near East. I'm told we've quite a force in Africa. Some two thousand men. Nobody knows, of course."

"You're saying they'll meet no opposition, then?" said the lieutenant. "Why any village leader could cope with these half-starved soldiers and fizz-brain staff rabble."

"The soldiers will carry it through," said Swinburne. "The thousand which have been on constant garrison duty here are also immune to soldier's sickness by the process of natural selection."

"They'll have eighteen hundred men," said the lieutenant.

"And we'll have nothing but a lingering death from boredom," said Carstair.

"Why didn't you chaps go with the other officers?" asked the lieutenant.

Swinburne looked uneasily across at Carstair and then shrugged. "We sound hopeless. We really aren't. My men, the whole hundred, depended upon me to stick by them. His men, about twenty, have done the same. We occasionally get a message through from our sergeant majors."

"And so you stick in the faint hope that you'll be given back your commands?"

"Yes," said Swinburne.

"They'll never be *given* back," said the lieutenant.

"What do you mean?" said both men sharply, with uneasy glances at the door. Hope had suddenly blazed in their faces.

The lieutenant went on about the task of cleaning his muddy boots.

The barracks had originally been intended to accommodate a thousand men and so there was ample room for two hundred and eight. But for all that the place was damp and gloomy and, to soldiers who had begun to depend upon mobility rather than barricade for protection, it was too near from wall to wall and, compared with the sky, too close from ceiling to floor.

A silence fell upon the Fourth Brigade as they went about preparing their abiding place. For the first few minutes they feverishly got things in order and then, that accomplished, they touched up themselves. But more and more, as the hours passed, they glanced inquiringly toward the door. Two or three times false word came that the lieutenant had arrived and there was a scurry of activity to make certain everything was all right. They supposed, naturally, that General Victor would accompany the lieutenant upon this inspection and, above all things, they did not want to disgrace their officer.

Bulger put dinner off and off until everyone was fairly starving, for he did not want to have the place messed up with food and smoke. Finally Pollard gave the word and Bulger's two scarecrows broke up some desks and benches to build a fire under the air outlet. There was another burst of activity to get supper through and cleared away before the inspection should come. And then, once more, they relapsed into waiting.

Little by little the tension died from them. They felt empty and neglected. They did not even know the time, for they no longer had the sky. A mild attack of claustrophobia was creeping over each of them.

In short, their morale was slipping. As long as they could remember, they had had the lieutenant in sight or alarm distance, and now that they did not know where he was, they felt nervous. What if something should happen? Of course, they knew nothing could happen, but still—

"An enemy command over that ridge, sir. About three hundred and fifty and machine guns."

"Weasel! Scout the position. Pollard, make sure we can march in ten minutes. Bulger, apportion those supplies. Carstone, are your guns in condition? Good. Stand by."

"Sir, there's damn near a regiment in that town."

"Pollard! Stand ready to feint a front attack. Hanley! Prepare to take cover on the right. Tou-tou! Your outfit take cover on the left. Carstone! Make ready an ambush. When Pollard sucks them out, roll up their flanks, cut their retreat and give Carstone his chance."

Yes, what if something should happen?

What if something *had* happened?

Gian went over his artillery again and wiped away some mythical dust and gave his men seven brands of Hades if they slipped up again.

"What you think, Gian?" said Tou-tou.

"How can I know what to think? These staff officers!"

"The sun's down. At least, those helios aren't working."

"He said he'd be back," said Gian.

"But he hasn't come back," said Tou-tou.

They wandered away from each other.

"Maybe he got sick all of a sudden," said Weasel. "Maybe he got sick and we weren't there!"

"Maybe they fed him some poison," said Bulger. "They know nothin' about food in a rat burrow like this!"

"Was he all right when you saw him last, Mawkey?" said Weasel for the thirty-second time.

"Yes," said Mawkey. "He'll be along. He hasn't seen those other officers for a long, long time and maybe he's sick of talking to stupid rabbits like us."

"Sure, that's it," said Bulger.

But nobody believed it.

There was another false alarm, and everybody eased down as soon as the noncom was clearly seen in the door. Nobody knew him, but as he was a sergeant major, Pollard received his greeting.

"I hear this is the Fourth Brigade," said the newcomer. "I'm Thomas O'Thomas of the Tenth Regiment, Second Brigade, Third Division, Tenth Army Corps." But when he said it he looked over his shoulder to see if anyone was listening. "That's the old outfit, of course," he added. "Major Swinburne commanding."

"'Orace Pollard, at your service. Second in command of the Fourth Brigade. Come in and have something."

"I *thought* that was food I smelled."

"Right you are," said Pollard, leading his guest

back to the square on the floor which was Pollard's office.

Thomas O'Thomas didn't miss anything as he came down the barrack. He saw haversack after haversack bulging with food and loot, belt after belt full of ammunition. This outfit was wealthy!

"And Heaven blind me!" said O'Thomas. "Artillery!"

"Yes-s-s, indeed," said Gian.

"There are some guns around here but they're shot out until a crew won't touch them. And these here weapons look like new."

Gian beamed happily and was greatly taken with Thomas O'Thomas.

Pollard seated his guest at the table and signaled to Bulger to have a man bring some barley soup and bark tea and real flour bread. O'Thomas could hardly believe his eyes and nose and, without apology, fell to with voracity.

"Some more?" said Pollard. "There's plenty."

"Plenty?" said Thomas O'Thomas.

"A bigger dish, Bulger."

Thomas O'Thomas slurped avidly through that and a third and then, scoffing off the tea with its liberal portion of beet sugar, felt that the age of miracles had returned.

"How do you manage it?" said Thomas O'Thomas.

"It's the leftenant," said Pollard. "He thinks of rations and bullets and the brigade, and nothin' else."

"Blind me! What an officer!"

"We picked this up in four days," said Pollard.

"Four— Aw, now, there ain't that much food in this whole bleeding country, chum."

"There is. That's the kind of commanding officer we got."

"We bloody well starved in the Tenth Regiment. That's why we came back here. But there ain't a thing to eat in this hole, let me tell you. And since they relieved Major Swinburne of his command, we never get nothing."

"They . . . they *what?*" cried Pollard, half on his feet.

"Why, certainly. Every time a field officer comes back to this rabbit warren, the staff takes away his troops and hands them over to some simpering mamma's boy that'd run forty miles if he ever heard a rifle cocked. And let me tell you, when you get your new officer you'll find out all about etiquette— saluting and playing nurse—" He found, suddenly, that he was surrounded by a group of tense faces belonging to all the noncoms of the organization. "Oh, I say, you chaps. You seem to be worked up!"

"What happened to your command officer?" said Pollard.

"Well, he was just relieved, that's all. We hated to lose him, because he was a fine man. A wonderful field officer and we all liked him. But what can we do? We haven't even been able to find out what happened to him."

"You haven't— See here!" said Tou-tou. "You actually let them take him away from you and never made a move to find him?"

"When we got it through our heads," said Thomas O'Thomas, "we were already broken up into other outfits. Just like you'll be. Wait and see. They'll spread you thin. That way there ain't no way you can give trouble." He felt uneasy, as though they didn't approve of him quite. "If you don't mind, now, I'll be going. I slid past the guard. Nobody is supposed to come here yet, you know."

"You mean we're isolated?" said Pollard.

"Well, call it that. They don't want anybody to start any trouble, you know." And so, bidding them farewell, Thomas O'Thomas left.

O'Thomas' going was the signal for the whole room to begin talking at once. Even the carriers, beasts of burden though they had been made by him, became anxious for the safety of the lieutenant lest they thereby receive a worse fate than having to eat well and work hard.

Before they had even started to get this talked out, two more high-ranking noncoms filtered in, on the alert for food. They were fed and they were pumped thoroughly.

"Look, you chaps," said one. "There's no use getting worked up. When the mutinies commenced they equipped all these barracks with regurgitant gas.

Calm down or you'll have it dumped on your heads."

Several more noncoms got through the guard and these added further confirmation.

"Your command officer?" said one. "Why, if he was a field officer, it's pretty plain what's happened to him. I'm from old Tin Can Jack's Hellfire Highlanders and I know. Tin Can Jack couldn't get us back three weeks ago and so he sloped."

"He ran away?" said the brigade, incredulous.

"And left you?" said Bulger.

"The whole blooming eighty-nine of us. He had to save his life, didn't he?"

"His life—" in horror.

"You ain't got any idea of these new staff officers," said the noncom from the Hellfire Highlanders. "You see, when they killed the last dictator in England and set up the B.C.P., it was General Victor what turned his coat and handed over the London garrison to the Commies. Him and all his officers. And when that was done, the B.C.P. had to do something for him and they was scared of him, because a traitor once may be a traitor twice and so they just shipped him over here with all his blinking officers to remove General Bealfeather. So they aren't nothing, these staff officers, but a lot of whipped cream and gold braid and they're scared of the field officers—"

And so it went throughout the night. The stores of the Fourth Brigade went rapidly down and their alarm went rapidly up. They paid good food for information, despite the repeated warning, sotto voce, that they wouldn't get such fare here in the garrison. They were too desperate to care.

And when morning came, finding them without sleep, they were at last quiet. At least, Malcolm found them so.

"Atten*shun!*" barked a noncom they hadn't seen before.

Captain Malcolm came in. He was freshly shaved and laundered and he carried a crop under his arm and wore gloves. He scowled when he saw that very few had come to their feet. He turned and beckoned in a picked squad of garrison soldiers. Sullenly, the Fourth Brigade stood up.

Malcolm looked them over, not very complimentary to their condition, or deportment, or weapons. Pollard followed him around more to keep him from doing anything than to aid his inspection.

At last Captain Malcolm came to the center of the room. He felt that he should make a speech.

"Soldiers," said Malcolm, "you are, of course, in very sorry shape." From what the Fourth had seen of the garrison, they did not believe it. "And your discipline, it is plain to see, has been very slack." There was a mutter and Malcolm glanced around to see if the garrison guard was handy and alert. "However, as soon as you are split up into your new organizations and your ranks filled from theirs, we shall go about improving you. As your commanding officer, I—"

"Beg pardon?" said Pollard.

Malcolm glanced back and was reassured by the garrison guard. "Sergeant major, if you wish to see the orders"—gently sarcastic—"I shall be glad to show them to you."

"The only orders we recognize," said the stolid Pollard, "are those that comes from the leftenant's mouth."

"Oh, now, see here, old man, I—"

"I said it and I'll stick by it. Call this mutiny or anything you like, but you ain't going to do anything to our leftenant!"

Malcolm backed a pace and then stiffened with anger. "I care to call it mutiny! Sergeant of the guard, arrest this man!"

"Touch him," said Tou-tou. "Just go ahead and touch him."

"And this man," said Malcolm, pointing to the burly Tou-tou.

"Sergeant of the guard," said Malcolm, "sound the alarm."

The clamor went screaming through the fortress.

"In a moment," said Malcolm, "we'll have an adequate force here. You will be relieved of your food and given strict confinement. Sergeant of the guard, take this brigade sergeant major in custody as well as his thick-skulled friend."

The sergeant hesitated a moment. But he heard

troops coming on the run and it looked like a cheap way to make face for himself. He advanced and laid a hand on Pollard.

A revolver cracked and smoke writhed from Hanley's fist. The sergeant caught at his guts and began to scream. The guards tried to get through the door and away but pinned themselves there by their very anxiety. Malcolm, white-faced, sought to claw through them.

A rifle blazed and the back of Malcolm's head came off, splattering the others in the door. Malcolm's arms kept on beating and then froze out straight.

Carstone's pneumatics began to pop like champagne corks and the blood began to flow. The door, in thirty seconds, was barricaded by the bodies of the garrison men.

Beyond, an officer leaped into view, not having heard the pneumatics in the roar of sound. He jerked and his hands flew to his chest and were full of holes.

Above them a powder began to flow out from automatic trips. The regurgitant.

"Clear away!" howled Gian. And the doorway was clear of the Fourth Brigade as far back as the artillery.

Three guns crashed as one, and half the wall went out, fragments spattering through the corridor to knock back the garrison troops.

Hastily snatching their packs and trying not

to breathe, the Fourth leaped into the corridor. Gian whiplashed the carriers into moving guns and caissons. Men were already beginning to gag and vomit.

Pollard's bellow brought eyes to him. He sorely missed his lieutenant but it was up to him and he had to act. He pointed up the least defended incline and they sped along it. Behind them Carstone's pneumatics were covering their retreat by hammering back the mob of garrison soldiers.

When the last of Gian's artillery rumbled by, Carstone began to have his machine guns shifted at intervals. By picking up the first of the string in rotation and making it the last, he was able to keep the corridor behind them sprayed and still retreat.

A clang sounded up again and Pollard began to howl for Gian. The artillery came up, the brigade hastily making room for it. A great steel door had dropped into place across the corridor and powder was again beginning to sift from above it.

"Stand back!" screamed Gian. "Ready guns three and four. Fire!"

The center of the door bulged out.

"Guns three and four reload! Fire!"

The bulge increased. The brigade was retching. Behind them the pneumatics sputtered and hissed, interspersed at intervals with the coughing clatter of the Belgian alcohol gun.

"Guns three and four! *Fire!*" bawled Gian.

The door collapsed. The half-deafened troops sped through it, some of them hastily binding wounds received from the ricocheting splinters of steel and stone.

Soon Pollard faltered in dismay. Quite evidently the corridor he had chosen had only gone up long enough to avoid a particularly hard seam of rock and then had been built downward. They were on their way into the depths of the fortress!

Wildly he glared about for another passage and found none. He had to go forward now. All the way through the place. Thank Heaven the regurgitant effect had been slight and was wearing away. Oh, if the leftenant were only here to tell them!

He sensed rather than heard or felt the machine gun which had hastily been thrown on a barricade to bar their way. Before he came to the turn he halted and piled up the men behind him. They were glad to stop and breathe better air.

"There's a machine gun up there, Gian."

"Right. Gun one, forward. Load solid. Make way, will you, Pollard?"

Gian laid the gun himself with the care of an artist. He yanked the lanyard and the roar was too great for them to hear the shot bounce off the far end of the turn. There was a scream of agony from the barricade around the curve.

"Weasel, mop up!" said Pollard.

Weasel and four men snaked forward. Twice their rifles crashed and then there wasn't any more sound at the barricade. The Fourth Brigade went forward.

The central offices were quite deserted save for one orderly who had risked all to rummage among the general's effects for any possible food cache. Pollard hurried into the offices and glanced about, hoping to find a map of the fortress. But the grenade they had tossed into the place first had ripped up the wall chart beyond recognition. The remaining orderly, who had taken cover behind a desk, was hauled forth. He clearly expected to have his throat cut.

"Soldier," said Bulger, sticking his bayonet into the orderly's ribs and tickling him up a bit, "if you want to live, you'll lead us straight as a bullet to our leftenant."

"Y-y-you are the Fourth Brigade?"

"Right."

"J-j-j-just f-f-f-follow m-m-m-me!"

They followed him. Evidently the garrison had had a full belly for they were not again obstructed. They drew up and tried to straighten their uniforms when they came to the indicated door.

Pollard knocked with his pistol butt.

The lieutenant opened it.

Pollard gave one of his very rare salutes, though he forgot to take the gun out of his hand first. "Sergeant major Pollard, sir. Fourth Brigade all present and accounted for. Will . . . will you please take command?"

It was very hard, just then, for the lieutenant to remember to keep full control of his emotions.

Burrowed like a rat with a phobia against hawks, General Victor and his staff received fragments of news and acted accordingly. Their first effort was to order out the garrison, en masse, to engulf and put to death the leaders of the mutineers. Very confidently, then, they huddled in the darkness, awaiting report of results. A full hour passed before any orderly came down to them.

It seemed that the loyal garrison was perfectly willing but that the field soldiers, while only half their number, were opposed.

General Victor frothed and spluttered and sent out orders again, even sending a staff major along with them. Half an hour went by before the staff major came back.

It seems that he had somehow blundered into the north barrack which had housed the Fourth and there had found the corpse of Captain Malcolm.

"Mutiny and murder!" howled Victor. "Get back up there and sweep them into cells!"

"That is the point, sir," said the staff major. "The garrison soldiers state they would be only too glad to do it but it seems, somehow, that their rifles are missing."

"What's this? What's this? Missing! Incredible!"

"It would seem so, sir, but you must not forget

that the field troops are quartered with the garrison troops now."

And so, bit by little, the staff pieced together the lieutenant's "fiendish" plan and their own defeat.

General Victor, once he understood, no longer raved. He just sat and stared at his boots in dumb dismay.

Smythe grew bitter, blaming everyone around him. "You should have understood! Why, I myself heard Captain Malcolm state his annoyance at the brigade's slow progress back. They attacked every possible source of food supply. It's plain now. He's the devil incarnate!"

An orderly came down, the same that had found the lieutenant for Pollard. He was happy to be momentarily free. "Sir, the compliments of the lieutenant and would the general come up under a flag of truce to discuss the terms?"

"Terms?" cried the officers. "For what?"

"Surrender, he says, sirs," apologized the orderly.

"Surrender! By all that ever *was* holy!" said Smythe. "Tell him no!"

"He says he'd hate to have to come down and get you, gentlemen. Begging your pardons."

"Come down— How perfectly ghastly!" Smythe grabbed the orderly by the coat and shook him. "Does he think he can take his own general headquarters? Does he?"

General Victor stood up wearily. "It appears that he has. I shall go speak with him."

They protested, but Victor did not hear them. Unwillingly they filed after him up through the fortress to the higher levels. It was with great surprise that they found the troops all out of the ground.

The rain had ceased for the time and small shafts of sunlight were cutting along the slopes, flicking over the remains of many an attack and sparkling in the water which clung to the bottoms of shell holes. Nearly eighteen hundred men were out here, variously disposed upon the flat expanse between the hills.

Victor's very large head turned this way and that, taking it all in. He saw that a machine-gun company was stationed in such a way as to command the expanse and that riflemen were posted so as not to interfere with the machine guns. It appeared very much as if the garrison was about to be executed to a man.

The staff's eyes were burned by the light, to which they were not accustomed. And their courage also burned very low, for they bethought themselves of the possibilities of firing squads. Their consciences, where field officers were concerned, were very, very bad.

Victor located the lieutenant seated upon a rock, surrounded by several noncoms and two other officers. With misgivings he approached.

The lieutenant stood up and bowed, smiling.

"See here," said Smythe, beginning without

preamble. "This is mutiny, murder and desertion; a hellish plot!"

"A plot?" inquired the lieutenant innocently.

"You know very well what it is!" said Smythe. "You cannot deny it. You stocked your men up with food and brought them here. You *knew* what effect that would have upon this garrison. You *knew* that when you ordered your men to revolt, there would be no hand to oppose them. This is a vile trick!"

"Perhaps, Colonel Smythe, perhaps. But you are wrong in saying that I ordered my men to revolt. That was not necessary, you know."

"Ah!" cried Smythe. "You admit it! You admit you came here on purpose to avenge your friends."

"Vengeance," smiled the lieutenant, "was not part of my plan. However, I might include it."

"How else," howled Smythe, "could it be?"

"We have very poor rifles, gentlemen. We had no rain cloaks, no sound boots. We had no baggage carts, no new-style helmets. We were short on good ammunition and only long on strategy. As soon as we have what we want we shall leave you to your regrets."

General Victor thrust Smythe aside. "According to international law, sir, you are a brigand."

"If we must have law," said the lieutenant courteously, "then let it be military law, by which you are a fool. Now please stand aside while we get on with this business."

Swinburne, Carstair, Pollard, Tou-tou and

Thomas O'Thomas all looked wonderingly at the lieutenant. They had had no inkling of this as a deliberate scheme, but now they saw it clearly. They saw it in terms of numbers and guns, and gasped at the realization that the lieutenant had captured the only existing fortress in this countryside, garrisoned by sixteen hundred men, with not the loss of one in all his own command. Their faces softened into gentle worship as they gazed upon their officer.

It took half the day to complete the business. What with every garrison soldier clamoring to be included in the lieutenant's ranks and therefore turning out every possible hiding place for the hoarded stores, the detail became enormous.

The lieutenant worked on. He took no soldier who had not had at least three years in the lines with a combat division. He took no soldier who thought there should be anything even faintly resembling a soldiers' council. And he did not even take all the field troops, for many of these were not fit for active service and would only have proved a burden.

At dawn of the following day, the organizations were made up. Five hundred and fifty troops were assigned to two sections, with the cream of the Fourth Brigade marshaled into a body of scouts under the direct control of the lieutenant. By order, the whole was to remain the Fourth Brigade, with two regiments and one artillery unit.

Drawn up on the expanse before the hill, the

soldiers stood rigidly under the lieutenant's inspection, only a fortress guard under Pollard being absent from the ranks. The Union Jack was absent and in its place was the standard of the Fourth Brigade.

The lieutenant was very thorough. Each man had a good pair of boots, a rainproof cape, a visored helmet, a semiautomatic rifle, a breastplate, three bandoleers of ammunition, a canteen, a bayonet, a sharp-sided spade, six grenades, a good overcoat, two uniforms of regulation British slate blue, and an adequate haversack. The baggage carts were brimming with spare ammunition and condensed food. The artillery unit now had eight pieces and sixty noncombatants to draw them.

The lieutenant finished his inspection.

"Major Swinburne, is the First Regiment ready to march?"

"Yes, sir."

"Ensign Carstair, is the Second Regiment ready?"

"Yes, sir."

"Orderly, recall Pollard and inform him he is to bring up the rear guard. Weasel, lead off with the vanguard. *Brigade! By squads, left! March!*"

In the ranks of the Hellfire Highlanders a bagpipe began to scream and wail, accompanied by three drums. Englishman, Scotsman, Irishman, Australian, Canadian, Frenchman, Finn, Pole, Belgian, Italian, Dane, Spaniard, Moor and Turk stepped out to the barbaric strain, the standard of the Fourth Brigade streaming out in the fore.

General Victor stood downcast upon the lip of the fortress, watching the command snake over a ridge and out of sight until the bagpipes, finally, had vanished into the distance.

"I was wrong," said General Victor. "There's reason, then, why a field officer should be treated well. Smythe, I would to Heaven we had kept him under our command."

"There's no use talking about it now," said Smythe bitterly. "That outfit is headed for England!"

"You . . . you think so?" said the startled Victor.

"I'm certain. Come, we owe it to London to tell them of this revolt and of the man that led it. This debt will yet be paid."

Chapter VI

Near the middle of November, just as dawn eased across the horizon, a strange and hostile fleet crept along the dreary fen lands from seaward toward Gravesend.

There were nearly fifty boats in all, boats which had nothing in common but their rigs. Culled by fishermen from the harbors of the north coast of France, the vessels were ex-anything but fishermen. Submarine chasers, admirals' barges, lifeboats, lighters, torpedo boats, motor-sailers and, in short, almost anything which would float and could be handled by two or three men. Their superstructures bore no resemblance to the original architectural designs. Without exception one or two masts rose up from the deck of each to which was affixed a patchwork of rags and booms to make up the crudest kind of sails.

Once these vessels had had a very warlike aspect and though, for years, this had been missing in favor of fishing, once again there was some semblance to the battle boats they had been. They were crudely armored along the gunwales with barricades of sandbags and scrap plate and even boards. On nine of them artillery was mounted behind adequate shields and eight of them were carrying machine guns of widely different types.

It was a very quiet flotilla, quietly slipping through the thick and swirling mists like a number of spirits from the deep come to land to beg back their lives.

Leadsmen chanted softly as they found their deeps and marks, and impressed French sailors sat glumly at their tillers, depending wholly on the lead and lookout for their course, so impenetrable was the fog, so treacherous the shoals.

Soldiers lounged behind the barricades, finishing a light breakfast and silent now that an action might begin soon. They did not think much about it, for they had gotten out of that habit in early youth. It was enough to know that there was much food in the hold and that the Lieutenant was up there in the lead, watching out for anything which might develop and plotting the downfall of England.

Fifteen English fishermen had been picked up and their vessel and catch commandeered. These were piloting with all their faculties, for they had no liking for these handy guns and the faces of such hardened veterans. At first they had been very reluctant and one vessel had grounded on a bar. Now that there were but fourteen of them, they did their work very well.

Mawkey was the only one who could keep the shore in sight. To all others it was wholly invisible save at rare instances. Indeed there was not much shore to see, only flat, endless swamps, different from the water only in that they did not move with the inshore breeze.

Abreast of the leading vessel were two others, forming a slight triangle. The flanking pair were motor-sailers, some forty feet in length and very lightly burdened to have a shallower draft. In these, to port and starboard of the lead respectively, were Carstair and Swinburne. In the admiral's barge which felt the way was the Lieutenant.

"Bottom at two and a half fathoms," said the leadsman. "Bottom at two. Bottom at three. Bottom at three and a half fathoms."

The English fisherman turned frightened eyes to the Lieutenant. "We're in the river proper now."

"Keep on to Gravesend," said the Lieutenant.

On crept the flotilla, feeling through fog so dense that even Mawkey could no longer find the shore. But the leads told their story to the fishermen. They were coming in with the tide, aided by a very slight breeze from the sea which had come with dawn. There was, as yet, no indication that the fog would lift at all, but the Lieutenant had his hopes.

It seemed so strange to be coming back. It was as though he had never been here at all, so filled his mind had become with five years of war, packed upon eighteen years of it. He recalled very little of the Thames, except that, in this time of year, the fog sometimes lifted for a little while in midmorning and then settled back for the entire day, and that these very marshes were the rising places of that fog. If he had calculated aright, they would be sighted only when they reached Gravesend.

If the gods of battle were kind—

They had nearly run down a great cliff which loomed high above them in the fog. Panic gripped the English pilots and orders ripped across the fleet. In a moment the cliff was plain and they were going around it.

A great battleship was here, solidly held up by mud. It had burned to the water and its plates were twisted and gaping. The turrets were all awry and half the guns had been blown away. The masts were trailing overside, eaten by rust and still clutched by the tattered dead. This had happened long ago and the name of the vessel was not decipherable.

In three hours the fog began to lift a little and the shores became dim outlines which gradually took form. They had timed their arrival well. Gravesend was to port, Tilbury to starboard.

There was not much left of Gravesend—a few

walls, a lonely stack, the bones of lighters upon the mud, a few vessels sunken at their wharves. The Royal Terrace Pier was a collection of stumps in the water. The ripraps which had held back the banks had given way here and there, spilling abandoned buildings into the river. The chalk hills which sloped up and away were denuded of trees and buildings alike, the whole having been consumed by fire. Not even a shrimp fisherman was here.

The flotilla wore about and approached Tilbury. And as they neared they found that the Tilbury Docks were not in better condition. A few stones marked where Tilbury Fort had stood. Only an ancient blockhouse, dating almost from Roman times, was whole and sound. Of the great deep-sea docks there was very little sign. Of the great petrol storage tanks there was nothing but a scorched area, which accounted for the burning of both the north- and south-bank cities, just as the absence of the government powder magazines higher up accounted for the collapse of the higher walls. This was all old to the Lieutenant, but it seemed as if he saw it for the first time. But there was one thing new. The river was cleaner than he remembered it and the fog less yellow.

As he had hoped, they were sighted from the shore, for a man went racing along the dike toward the blockhouse. And, a moment later, several other men came streaming forth to see for themselves.

The flotilla picked its way among the bars which

had formed from the lack of dredging and the breaking, here and there, of the dike. Two large freighters were decaying, held fast by the rising bars, unable to make the sea as they had made the shore. But they were too far out for the Lieutenant's purpose.

Some distance west of the blockhouse he brought the flotilla to anchor, parallel with the shore and a hundred yards or so out from the nearest tide flat. The sulphury odor of tidewater grass was strong in their nostrils.

The Lieutenant examined the beach. It afforded very slight cover anywhere within rifleshot save for the remains of a few boats. And as the only sound ones of these appeared to be wrecked destroyers out of some attacking fleet, it was highly unlikely they would be out of the water at high tide. The place suited him.

The anchor lines of the small vessels stretched out taut with the tidal current, broadside to the beach. They were perfectly quiet.

Before long a considerable force came floundering along the partially inundated marsh. The Lieutenant estimated them as numbering around six hundred. For the moment he was made to wonder, for it did not seem likely that such a number would be kept at Tilbury.

The tide still exposed a long bar and down this came a commander with three staff officers and a twenty-man guard. The commander halted with arms akimbo, the faint wind in his cape, staring at the leading boat.

"Where from?" he bellowed.

"France!" replied the Lieutenant. "The Fourth Brigade coming home!"

There followed a brisk consultation and then the commander hailed the fleet again. "Turn back! We have orders to annihilate you if you attempt to land."

Swinburne and Carstair, in their vessels close by the Lieutenant's, were shocked to see a happy grin suffuse their leader's face. "For what reason?"

"We have been advised," bawled the commander, "by General Victor's headquarters that you have mutinied. We want nothing to do with Continental soldiers! Turn back or we'll fire upon you."

"Carstone!" shouted the Lieutenant. "Kill me those officers!"

Carstone, in the fourth boat, bawled an order to his gunners with the range.

Instantly three machine guns began to spit and cough. The tide flat was churned by ripping slugs. The shore officers had whirled and raced madly toward their troops, but before they had gone twenty yards they were hammered down and sent rolling. In less than thirty seconds there was nothing alive on the spit.

"Cease firing!" said the Lieutenant.

Higher up the gathered troops, seeing the dead bodies of their leaders, leaped into activity, scooping out foxholes and throwing themselves down to begin a hysterical fire upon the ships. But they could see no targets behind those barricaded gunwales, and though the water frothed and steel clanged with the fury of the fusillade, little harm was done and no fire came from the vessels.

There was a lull. Messengers could be seen dashing away across the marshes to the west, obviously heading for London with a plea for reinforcements. And still no fire came from the fleet. The boats lay in the hazy sunlight, apparently asleep.

Both Swinburne and Carstair were aghast at the wanton execution of the shore officers, not because men had died, but because of the result which was inevitable. Every man available, every gun which could be fired would be rushed to this place to wipe them out of existence. Such a maneuver would outnumber them and make it quite impossible to effect a landing. For once it was obvious that the Lieutenant's luck was not holding, or else that his hopes of being received peaceably had gone glimmering with the replacement of rage for wisdom.

The fire from shore slackened for lack of targets and had almost ceased when the Lieutenant gave another order: "One rifleman each vessel snipe the shore."

The fire was deadly, for cover on the beach was sparse. Madly the troops there strove to deepen their foxholes, many dying before they could achieve it. Further messengers went snaking off through the marsh grass toward London.

The result was a wild increase in firing from shore. As soon as it became dangerous to return it from the boats, another order was passed:

"Cease firing."

Two men had been wounded in the arms out of the Fourth Brigade. At least thirty-five were casualties ashore.

The mist began to settle slowly down into fog once more as the morning waned. But thick as it got, each time the firing ashore slackened, the Lieutenant aggravated it anew. Hits were few under such conditions, for men were visible only when they moved on shore and the boats were only darkly furled sails connected by a shadow with the water.

The corpses on the sand bar were carried upriver as the tide rose and, some hours later, came bobbing back to trail along the hulls and fade into the fog toward the sea.

The day went slowly. Protected by the steel hulls or the barricaded decks, the Fourth Brigade was served hot meals on time, was relieved in orderly fashion, and told themselves and each other that this was the real way to conduct a war.

Night came. A few alarms clove the fog. A few random shots howled away from the steel plates. The Fourth Brigade changed its watches and speculated on how the Lieutenant might possibly crack this landing problem.

Dawn came, lighting up the fog but doing little for visibility. The morning wore on and the fog began to lift.

When they could again see the shore, they found that the troops there had dug themselves a deep trench which, though it certainly must be half full of water, afforded good protection from the boats. The routine of the former day went on, with the boats prompting the shore fire each time the latter showed signs of slackening. Three more casualties were suffered in the fleet, one of them fatal by reason of a Frenchman taking off his helmet to see the dent a bullet had placed in it.

There seemed to be a considerable augmentation of forces on the beach, but, at the same time, there seemed to be less enthusiasm in the shooting. The brigade, war-wise, read this as a very bad sign.

"Mawkey," said the Lieutenant when the clear period was thickening into a London special, "keep your eye peeled upriver. They may try to float troops down on us with the ebb of this tide."

Other lookouts were posted and the routine of the day settled down to chance shooting and hot meals and speculation. The tide had ceased to make about eleven. The Lieutenant went below, or at least into the after cockpit, and played solitaire with a greasy pack of cards.

Swinburne had his boat hauled astern the

admiral's barge and came aboard, and Carstair, crossing Swinburne's craft, also came aboard.

They sat down and watched the Lieutenant play, occasionally indicating something they thought he might miss in building on his aces.

"Lieutenant," said Swinburne at last, "we have every confidence in you. Your feats of getting these boats and the supplies for them, your additions to our artillery all speak for themselves. But we believe that if we are to land we should do it on the opposite bank, where there is no force."

"Every confidence?" smiled the Lieutenant. "Captain Swinburne, I may miss a trick or two in solitaire, but I never miss a trick in battle. I at least hope I don't. Let them collect their forces and alarm the countryside. This is one of those rare moments when we can relax. Our men have food and are happy. We have good, dry beds. We have just finished a most harrowing sea voyage in cockleshells. Let us rest."

"But to fight such a tremendous force as will collect—" began Carstair.

"We are good soldiers," said the Lieutenant. "I haven't heard you howl about odds yet, Carstair."

Swinburne and Carstair were uncomfortable. They took their leave and returned to their boats.

About two thirty, Mawkey set up a clamor, pointing excitedly upstream. The Lieutenant came up and peered through the thickness. Presently he could make out the hulls of boats drifting down upon them.

"Gian!" cried the Lieutenant through cupped hands. "Mortars on those vessels and don't miss!"

Gian's men were already standing to their guns on the various gunboats. Gian barked the range and elevation and fuse set. Artillerymen dropped their bombs into the muzzles of the mortars.

The drifting vessels were almost upon them. A furious fire lashed out from both sides and the fog was ripped by machine-gun slugs and grenades.

The mortar fire was deadly, bursting three or four feet off the packed decks of the attacking vessels and clearing the crews away from the small-bore rapid-fires before a brigade boat was even hulled.

Crouched behind their barricades, brigade grenadiers looped accurate incendiary grenades into the drifting craft when they were scarcely more than visible. Flame geysered among the ranks of the attackers. The fog was blasted again and again by the mortars. Shrapnel and solid shot finished their task. Less than twenty shore troops boarded and these were immediately killed. Against such experienced veterans they indeed had but little chance.

Men struggled in the water, carried past the flotilla by the tide and so out to sea.

The battle had lasted four minutes by the barge chronometer. The only survivors of the attacking party were the eight who were hauled up for questioning and those few who had managed to swim ashore. Brigade casualties amounted to three killed and seven wounded.

The Lieutenant took a prisoner below for questioning, and the man's nerves were so badly unstrung that he answered readily, if disconnectedly.

"What kind of government, if any, do you have?" said the Lieutenant.

"The B.C.P.," replied the soldier.

"How long have these Communists been in power?"

"A year, two years, three years— You'll kill me when this is done?"

"Not if you answer properly. Who is the leader?"

"Comrade Hogarthy. But there are many other leaders. They quarrel. But Comrade Hogarthy has the greatest power. Almost all the country is in his control—or the army, I mean."

"How many men in your army?"

"Six thousand."

"And your headquarters?"

"The Tower of Freedom."

"What's that?"

"It was the Tower of London. Most of it is still standing."

"How much artillery do you have?"

"I . . . I don't know. Some in the Tower of Freedom, I think. Some three-inch. Hogarthy took what big guns were left and had them destroyed, except for those he kept. There isn't much ammunition."

"Can you swim?"

"Sir? I mean, yes."

"Then swim ashore with the message that if Hogarthy will surrender unconditionally to me I won't attack his army there on shore. Repeat that."

The soldier repeated it.

"Now swim," said the Lieutenant.

The soldier, not believing he was still alive, hauled off his crude shoes and ill-fitting jacket with its red tabs and dived over the side to presently vanish in the fog.

"Mawkey."

"Yessir."

"That calls for a drink."

"Yessir."

And the Lieutenant, smiling happily, leaned back upon the admiral's cushions and shuffled his cards.

Chapter VII

Shortly before dawn, Weasel and Bulger pulled their dripping selves over the gunwale of the admiral's barge and sent word of their arrival to the Lieutenant. He was seated in the stern cockpit with a map of the Thames spread out upon his knees, checking over river obstructions with an English fisherman.

The Lieutenant looked up and raised the candle a trifle. He sent the fisherman away and scanned the pair amusedly. "I never thought," he said, "that I would live to see the day when Bulger bathed, but now I can die content."

Bulger, with brown river water forming a pool about his feet as it cascaded over his protruding stomach and dropped, grinned happily to be noticed so. He hefted a bag made out of a rubber poncho.

"We thought maybe the Lieutenant would want

to know what the shore over there looked like," said Weasel, "but this pelican wouldn't be content unless he brought back half their rations."

"I wondered whether you could stand the temptation," said the Lieutenant. "I sent Hanley ashore about two hours ago to reconnoiter, but he hasn't returned."

"Then we'll be first with the news," said Weasel. "Sir, they got about four thousand men over there now and they've brought up six small field pieces, maybe six-pounders, and they've made a barricade out of one of them destroyers when the tide was low last night. They're gettin' ready for a party and we're the guests of honor."

"Any estimate of their ammunition?"

"Sure," said Bulger. "There ain't any limit."

"What?"

"It's this way," said Weasel. "Y'see, they evidently run out of shells and so they got the breeches of these guns sealed. They load them from the muzzle with a rammer, usin' plenty of black powder and some fuzzy-lookin' stuff for wadding. Then they put chunks of this and that in the guns and they got artillery. I figure maybe they got bigger stuff up the river that they use the same way. Remember them guns that used to be park ornaments? Them that didn't have no breech you could open? Well, I figure maybe they're usin' those the same way. Damnedest way to use a gun I ever heard of."

"Muzzle-loaders," said the Lieutenant thoughtfully. "Weasel, I'm afraid we've got some work cut out here. Look." He took a pencil and drew a picture of an old demi-cannon, remembered from military history. "This is the touchhole. They put a length of fuse in it and light it and it goes through and touches off the powder. Then they stop the vent when the gun goes off. They've probably bored holes in their modern artillery so that they can touch it off in this fashion."

"But why do they do that?" complained Bulger.

"Because the rifling in those guns must be worn out and because it takes lots of machinery to make shells. And they're using black powder because any cadet could make it out of the materials at hand. This is very serious. Those things could blow us out of the water."

"They must have had an awful time getting that stuff across the marshes there," said Weasel. "The dike is gone in lots of places and it's just like a sea in there."

"Well, look," said the Lieutenant. "The way you put a cannon like this out of commission is to drive a spike into the touchhole."

"Yeah?" said Weasel, excitedly. "Hell, sir, we can do that before it gets light. Come on, Bulger—"

"Slowly," said the Lieutenant. "We aren't going to do anything like that for yet a while. Let them have their guns. What kind of troops are there ashore?"

"Pretty awful," said Bulger. "But at eight to one they can afford to be. They evidently hauled every farmer around here down and put a rifle in his hands."

"Then these aren't Hogarthy's regulars from London?" said the Lieutenant.

"They don't look like any regulars I ever saw," said Weasel.

"Well—we'll just have to wait," said the Lieutenant.

"Huh?" said Bulger. "You mean you're too proud to fight this rabble? Why, we could knock them kicking if we make a night attack. But if we wait for them regulars, if they exist—"

"Thank you, Bulger."

"Aw, I didn't mean nothin', sir. You know your business and if you say fly to the moon, we'll fly to the moon, sir. You know that."

"The greater the force," said the Lieutenant, "the greater the odds, the greater the victory." He smiled at them. "Now get back to your boats."

Bulger opened the pack and laid some buns on the Lieutenant's table, along with some slices of ham. Hurriedly, then, they got out.

The Lieutenant stepped to the deck and watched them over. It was plain to him that the tide was flooding, the way they struggled to breast it. He eyed his fleet, but all he could see were the vessels of Swinburne and Carstair, the first rather plainly, the second very dim. What fog this autumn brought!

"Pollard," he said.

Pollard came tumbling up from the forward cockpit. "Sir?"

"Pass the order that the flotilla is to move two miles up the river and anchor there. No noise. Just drift with the tide and steer with sweeps."

Hanley came up over the barricade along the gunwale like some monster out of the deep. He was very excited. "Sir, they've got—"

"Guns," said the Lieutenant. "Six of them. Give me your report later, but right now slip below and get dry."

Hanley blinked and then glanced distrustfully ashore. But nothing could be seen but fog. Mystified, he slid into the forward cockpit.

Quietly the flotilla got under way, carried by the flooding tide. As quietly they anchored two miles upstream. And when the morning clear period came and the shore gunners were about to blow a fleet to splinters, the fleet was no longer there. Officers fumed and raved until a runner came sprinting up with the information that the flotilla was anchored again two miles upriver. Instantly order was regained. Men unblocked the field pieces and loaded baggage on their backs and slogged west. They met no opposition from the fleet and they supposed it to be low on ammunition. That it had stopped was almost certain proof that it had chosen another place for the battle.

The camp had been only partly moved when another maneuver occurred to worry them. Four vessels detached themselves from the fleet and sailed away, evidently headed across the river. The fog had closed before the field pieces could be brought into action. But they had been set up and now, without warning, shells began to thunder out from the flotilla and tear into the batteries, even though the latter were wholly invisible.

Gian stayed behind while the fleet poled itself two more miles upstream, and then Gian, tired of firing at targets he could only hope he was hitting, also had his gunboats moved, bringing up the rear against the set of the water.

About one, the sound of firing was heard far across the stream. Instantly the camp was again in turmoil. Word was swiftly sent to head off any troops which might be on their way down and redirect them over the river to cover the opposite bank.

But, about two, the firing ceased. The four vessels which had been detached for water came back to report a successful landing which had been wholly unresisted, but that their scouts, about three thirty, had heard boats crossing upstream and had supposed that troops were being landed on the other bank. The Lieutenant ordered the water to be distributed, a fifty-gallon drum to each three vessels, and sat down to calmly enjoy a cup of tea.

Not until the following predawn did he have

another report on the shore troops. Weasel, strictly ordered not to touch the shore artillery if any of it had survived Gian's bombardment, brought the news that another complete army had arrived, bringing with it even more field pieces. There were now, he said, about eight thousand men swarming on both banks.

The Lieutenant gave his orders. There was a little wind, nominally from the northeast but turned east by the river channel. It was just enough to carry the fog of the marshes continually up to London. The flotilla made no effort, today, to be quiet. Booms creaked and canvas slatted and sweeps groaned. In the foggy dark, they offered no targets, though the shore troops began to light up the world before the sun with a wild fanfare of shooting. They had gotten their batteries moved again and now the air shrieked as slugs and rocks and pieces of pipe sought blindly for a mark. A mosquito boat was hit and sunk without casualty beyond its ammunition and food, for the crew grabbed hard to the next boat in line. A sailor lucklessly stopped a chunk of boiler plate which cut him half in two.

The fire was not returned. Already the flotilla was drawing away into the channel and driving west toward Woolwich at an average speed of four knots over the ground.

Leadsmen chanted loudly. Soldiers talked from boat to boat. And occasionally the Lieutenant passed the word to various craft to fire a few shots in the direction of either bank. It was a very noisy passage.

When the clear period came they found they had overshot Woolwich. Not that there was much of value there, for the arsenal, in blowing up long ago, had taken half the town with it. Shooters Hill was far behind. But there was evidence of a battery on the docks with new works, and the Lieutenant had Gian throw a few mortars back at it for luck.

The wind strengthened, which was fortunate, for the tide was nearly at flood, and the fleet jibed around the great horseshoe bend, passing hard by the Isle of Dogs. Navigation was difficult here, for the Greenwich Hospital had been blown down so thoroughly that great chunks of masonry had aided in the building of shallow bars.

Two shore batteries, constructed amid the ruins of the West India Docks to one side and the Surrey Commercial Docks on the other. But, having seen them from afar, Gian silenced them before the flotilla was in range of the shore guns, and all that was received in passing came from rifles.

From here to Greenwich the going was swift despite the turned tide, for the wind was on the quarter and the flotilla sped along at six knots over the water.

The fog had dropped heavily again when they turned at Greenwich to go in a northerly direction toward London. The wind had also dropped and the haul up was slow so that it was very late when they at last dropped anchor in the Limehouse Pool.

They did not announce their anchorage with any sound whatever, but quietly went about supper, wondering what the Lieutenant would do next. It was, however, rather plain that he meant to make an attack upon the Tower either tonight or at dawn.

At nine that night, the Lieutenant detached the First Regiment's Second Company under Swinburne's direction and sent them in five vessels to land in the Causeway. They had orders to construct a barricade in a likely place, to march west and make contact with the Tower and then retreat full speed to the barricade where Carstone would cover their embarking, after which they, in the boats, were to cover Carstone's departure.

The Lieutenant sat in the after cockpit and played solitaire. From time to time he lifted his head and listened, but as yet no firing had begun. He knew that Limehouse was a mass of rubble, having burned eighteen years ago, nine years ago and seven years ago, after each rebuilding. After the third time, it had been abandoned. The going would not be good and he did not expect the regiment back before one or two in the morning. He dozed through his games and waited.

Sharp firing suddenly broke out upriver. Knowing that it would be wholly impossible to see anything in this fog and dark, the Lieutenant dealt himself another hand. The firing slackened, picked up and then settled down to an even exchange. A boat grated against the admiral's barge.

Mawkey thrust his head into the cockpit. "Weasel is here to see you, sir."

"Bring him down."

Weasel was very well spent. Up on deck two or three of his soldiers could be heard examining their blisters in low tones.

"Where have you been?"

"You know what you said, sir, about them cannon?"

"Yes."

"Well, you told me I could scout the shore if I wanted."

"Yes?"

"I hope you won't get sore, sir, but I come on a battery of them things and we spiked them."

"Where?"

"Just about at the place where Big Ben used to be, sir."

"You've been all the way up there?"

"Yessir, and it was an awful hard row."

"What's London look like?"

"It's all inside the Old Roman Wall, sir, just like I seen it last. They built it up quite a bit in there. Must be thirty or forty thousand people in the place, mostly living on top of the ground now."

"Carry on, Weasel."

The Lieutenant started to deal another hand when Hanley was ushered down. His hands were also raw from pulling at sweeps, for he had been dropped off with another soldier and a fisherman at Greenwich and the row had been long.

"I come to report, sir."

"Anything downriver now?"

"They must have sent a bunch of boats and soldiers down to catch us because I passed them downriver about three hours ago. Missed us in the dark, I guess. I had an awful time finding you, even with those orders you gave the fisherman."

"What else?"

"About five hundred men were heading east through Greenwich. I made contact with them. It was easy to do because they've been scraped up and hardly knew each other. I also seen that main body's vanguard. They were all splattered with mud and lather and about wore out, but they was heading up to London and I guess the main body is right behind them, following the river. They'll be up here by tomorrow morning, guns and all."

"Very good, Hanley. Carry on."

The Lieutenant thoughtfully shuffled his deck. Time was dragging and he leaned back to catch forty winks, knowing he would awaken as soon as the tone of the firing changed.

He did. Carstone's machine guns started up about twelve thirty and continued for fifteen minutes in short, careful bursts. Then, one by one, the guns stopped, the shooting taken up by rifles. After a little the rifles faded out and the night was quiet.

The Lieutenant came on deck and ordered

Pollard to call out to the returning boats, giving them an accurate bearing.

Presently Swinburne, with his empty sleeve ripped, his face dark with powder and dirt, and his one eye blazing with battle, came aboard.

"We brought them all the way back to Limehouse, Lieutenant. And we left them jumping up and down and swearing purple."

"Casualties?"

"We suffered three dead and nine wounded, two of them seriously. All officers returned safely." He took the glass Mawkey was handing him and drained it thankfully. "We must have cut them up pretty badly, though there was nothing to shoot at but rifle fire and we used pneumatics as much as we could. Whatever it was for, it came off very well."

"Very good, Swinburne. You'd better get back to your boat and see to it. Pollard, check the redistribution of the troops and stand by to weigh anchor in fifteen minutes."

"Yessir."

"We're bound upriver," he said to Swinburne.

"Then you're not going to attack the Tower?" said Swinburne. "They've built it up again, but I think we could do it. If we'd thrown the Second Regiment west of that place, we could have had it tonight when we sucked the garrison out."

"Carry on, Swinburne. Orders, Pollard."

The Lieutenant went below and turned in, instantly asleep.

Chapter VIII

All that night the flotilla eased slowly upriver. The fore part was spent in locating and skirting the remains of fallen bridges and sunken vessels, with no slightest glimpse of the shore or sky to aid them. A gunboat went so solidly aground that t had to be unloaded, its mortar transferred and the craft fired. Behind them the blaze was but a dull glow which turned the pea soup faintly red. Firing was heard in that direction, interspersed by the occasional thunder of a larger gun. But evidently the river in general and not the flotilla was the target, for nothing came near.

With the morning came a heavy, cold rain which somewhat dispelled the haze for all its wetness, and the brigade found itself far upriver from London, in fact, approaching the half-tide lock just below Richmond.

Soldiers swathed in their rainproofs looked questioningly at the barrier. The tide was later here and it was just passing into the second half of the flood. Along the footbridge of the lock, which was in repair, a small force was gathering, evidently the garrison of some nearby fortress. Others were dragging two field pieces down the slope from the terrace but these, as yet, were far off.

When the flotilla came to within two hundred yards of the lock, both sides opened fire. But orders went swiftly back and the last six boats, under the command of Tou-tou, eased in to the shore and unloaded. Gian was impatient, but he knew his fire would damage the lock.

Tou-tou wasted no time in his attack. He curved far out through the heavy brush and formed his line. The garrison immediately drew up there, only to be raked from the flank by a merciless fire from Carstone and two mortar shots from Gian. Tou-tou swept up and through and, tossing bodies away from the runway, opened the lock and guarded the flotilla through. Sergeant Chipper took twenty men and lanced up the slope to capture the field pieces which he destroyed.

Once through, the flotilla paused, anchoring in midstream, until Tou-tou, under orders, mined and destroyed the lock. And even then they did not go on, but lay at lazy anchor, watching downstream.

About four, the vanguard of the shore forces put in an appearance about half a mile downriver, word of which was hastily brought to the fleet. But the Lieutenant was in no hurry. He waited until the vanguard was within shelling range and then had Gian drop two mortars into them. The vanguard hastily drew back. In half an hour the main body was seen, skirting Terrace Hill as though to cut off the flotilla from the upriver side. Two more mortars were dropped by way of promise and the flotilla, taking advantage of the very strong wind which had sprung up with the thickening of the rain, upped sail and continued west, past Richmond, and around the S bend which led to Kingston.

The wind slacked down with the rain, and clouds began to scurry, belly to earth. The low-pressure area was somewhere in their vicinity and the wind they got now was very uncertain, constantly shifting. Visibility thickened as the day faded. The rain stopped entirely at dark and it seemed to the shore forces that the stage was set for an ideal battle in their favor. They sent patrols up with the dusk and these met a very strong fire. The shore troops then got their artillery into position in the woods and scurried about, gaining the ire of every farmer in the surrounding countryside for their destruction of fences for barricades.

At seven o'clock the shore batteries opened up into the black and churned the river expanse before Twickenham where the fleet had anchored. They were very thorough about it, supplementing the guns with machine-gun fire. A force, meanwhile, scoured the banks for a mile both ways, getting everything that would float and then manning barges and lighters and rowboats with all the weight they would take.

They were certain now that the fleet was short on ammunition for no fire answered them and they knew that a force without many bullets will wait until the last possible moment.

Valiantly they launched their attack upon the inky river. Twice or thrice they fired on their own boats. They drifted with the current for a little way and then combed back. They set up excited, angry yells.

The flotilla was gone!

It had not passed Teddington pound lock.

It had not made the shore.

They abandoned their leaky vessels in favor of firmer land and hastily began to rake the countryside and shores for any sign of the Fourth Brigade.

They found none.

With sweeps and sails and current, but all in the heaviest of silence, the flotilla sped through the night, downstream to London. Past hamlet and bar, point and ruined castle they swept on their way.

And by four of the following morning, having negotiated wrecked bridges and derelicts and spits, they dropped quiet anchors just off the Tower but all the way across the pool. They were not lazy now but keyed to high pitch for the coming action.

The gunboats were disposed above and below

the fortress, out of range of the land batteries but within range for their own guns. Some forty boat-loads, then, hastily checking their equipment for the last time and memorizing their duties, warped in to the shore and effected a swift but silent landing amid the debris of buildings and wharves.

The Lieutenant, muffled in his cloak and helmet, crouched in the cover of a pile of stone and waited. Three-quarters of his forces, or three hundred and sixty men, were silent in the rubble-strewn dark about him.

It lacked about an hour of dawn and, with the usual consistency of London weather, a few stars were trying to shine in the murk. It would be a reasonably clear day.

Presently, to the east of the Tower, firing began. Swinburne had engaged the garrison as he had once before. And it was a startled garrison which tumbled from their bunks to snatch rifles and form inside the newly made east entrance. A sortie was made, driving the attacker back. And the raiding party seemed to be just as afraid to come to terms this time as it had the last.

The battle drew slowly away to the eastward, toward Limehouse. Reinforcements went out to settle the business once and for all. And when the garrison's sortie was nearly a mile from the Tower, its officers were dismayed to hear artillery upon the river which, by its sound, was certainly not their own, but good guns.

The Lieutenant crouched low. He could make out his gunboats now and he knew that Gian had the range. Solid shot was blasting away at the Middle Tower, the outermost rampart. The gate crumpled and, as though Gian had counted its bolts and measured its thickness with exactness, he wasted not one shot too many upon it. He transferred his fire to the Byward Tower, firing so as to blast any gate which might be there. Then he shifted two mortars and dropped a savage spray of shrapnel into the Outer Ward.

Without waiting for Gian to finish the job, the Lieutenant leaped up and waved his troops forward. They rushed through the Middle Tower and across the damaged bridge. The gate of the Byward Tower needed a grenade to finish the bursting of its lock and then they were in the Outer Ward. Gian had already begun to drop shells into the Inner Ward, having shelled the gate east of the Wakefield Tower until it could be breached. A few shots were fired down from the Bloody Tower as the troops rushed by, but as the defenders had to lean out to aim, they were dropped before they had gotten more than two men.

The Lieutenant scrambled over the rubble of the gate and leaped down into the Inner Ward. The mortars had cleared away here, and now all that was left was the White Tower.

Just as bombs had failed to destroy it, Gian's artillery could make but little dent upon this ancient

Norman keep, for its walls were fifteen feet thick. But there were doors and windows on those walls and now grenadiers came up with their bags of grenades, exploding one after another against the door. It gave ever so little under the onslaught.

Soldiers were firing down from the Tower now that Gian had stopped shelling. Snipers in the Fourth began to take their toll of the remaining defenders.

The Lieutenant saw that they were balked. He ordered the snipers to cover the slots and the bulk of his troops to withdraw to the Outer Keep. Then, gathering up a heavy bag of grenades, he rushed to the door, pulled the pin of one and chucked the whole into a slight break near the bottom. He swept around the side of the wall and pressed himself against it.

In a moment the grim old courtyard was torn with the thunder of this concerted explosion. The brigade yelled and dashed forward across the pavement.

They were within the keep and dashing toward the upper floors when a machine gun met them from a landing. Half a squad dropped. Grenadiers came to the fore and succeeded in pitching up a grenade to silence the gun.

Up swarmed the assault party. Each landing found a few defenders, but these, too, were vanquished.

In twenty-three minutes of attack, according t
Gian's chronometer, the Tower of London ha
passed into the hands of the raiders.

But there was no Hogarthy. A shivering staf
informed the Lieutenant that Hogarthy had gon
with the main garrison, up the river in pursuit o
the elusive gunboats.

But the Lieutenant was not disappointed. H
liked it that way. And when he had had a breathe
and a glass of ale from Hogarthy's special stock, sit
ting the while in Hogarthy's chair of office in th
frowning old room, he began to issue his command
again.

Swinburne had stopped running when the fir
ing had begun from the river and had let the gar
rison run into a gantlet of fire which brought then
to swift surrender. And, having worked so hard t
take them, he was astonished indeed when the Lieu
tenant ordered him to take them outside the walls
to place but three men over them and thereby le
them escape.

It was done. And the soldiers fled west towar
Hogarthy's forces.

Meantime the boats were unloaded and th
Fourth Brigade assigned to barracks in the old tow
ers. They were fed and allowed to rest, except fo
those under Weasel, who had gone out to contac
Hogarthy's vanguard a mile or two from town
when Hogarthy appeared.

The Lieutenant drank another glass of Hogarthy's special ale and broke out his pack of cards.

What happened to Hogarthy is history. How he floundered eastward through the mud, in haste to contact the invaders before they could repair the gates and walls and so entrench themselves. How he camped at dusk some three miles from Tower Hill, well aware that his troops, fagged out from days of stumbling along the river bank, must have rest.

The sortie which sucked Hogarthy out of that camp before he could even get his troops fed was led by Carstair, who battled back through the dusk to Tower Hill with every evidence of panicked flight.

The place where the battle was fought was well chosen by the Lieutenant, for it was flanked all around, at that time, with the wreckage of great buildings while the center was reasonably clear. It was into this that Gian dropped a murderous mortar fire and across this that Carstone swept his guns. Those facts in themselves would have accounted for Hogarthy's defeat.

But the main cause was weariness. Hogarthy's rabble had been whipped by their own Father Thames, and when they came to battle they were so exhausted that they cared not whether they stayed, or died, or fled. When the Lieutenant closed upon them from the west, from the very direction to which so many tried to flee, all fight was knocked out by the mere sight of a solid barrier of rifle fire.

Hogarthy was dug out of a swamp two days later and dragged into the Tower by an exuberant Bulger.

The town, however, had already paid its homage to the Lieutenant and the countryside all about was anxiously sending food to make peace with this fox of a conqueror.

"I've got Hogarthy below," said the excited Bulger. "All the people we met said it was him!"

"Good," said the Lieutenant, glancing up from a pile of documents. "Shoot him."

"Yessir," replied Bulger, speeding away.

Chapter IX

For years the soldier government ran smoothly, holding sway over England and Wales. A steady, calculating hand dealt adequately with the redistribution of the land and rehabilitation of the towns, for what war had failed to do, the Communists had done by way of wrecking any semblance of social system.

There were seven hundred and fifty thousand people within the Lieutenant's boundaries and, if fully half of these were under twenty, the restoration of central power was only made the easier by making old forms not only obsolete but also unknown.

The government took its taxes in tenths of production and upon the basis of stores held against emergency was able to issue a scrip which was valued as being backed by food. Government police were maintained by their posts and any political abuses were quickly stopped because they could be quickly reported.

Most of the work was directed at the land, very little of it toward manufacturing beyond the clearing out of certain sites to improve the appearance of the country. Youth was avid in its studies and though most of the libraries had been burned by bombs and Commies, there was still enough printed data to supply the working background of a very elementary kind of civilization.

The first great problem which jolted the Lieutenant was the amazing intricacy of industry. At first there was some talk of opening a clothing factory, but this led to the necessity of repairing a foundry, which meant that a smelter had to be run, which finally ended, not in the field with flax, but in the mines with iron and coal. It was given up. A few handicrafters had been able to set up some hand looms which were fairly efficient, even though built out of bedsteads and rifles and tractor parts. Three districts swiftly came to be employed for clothing and blankets, and as the government took its tenth and, in turn, made it possible for the weavers and tailors to eat and keep warm, everyone was happy.

Of building stone there was no lack. But the forests, destroyed far back by incendiary bombs along with the cities, furnished nothing but scrub saplings. And so youth became clever with stone.

A treaty was early concluded with the man who styled himself King of Scotland, for animals were to be had there but gunpowder and coal were not. Hence, a rather interesting trade was begun by sea.

The Thames' influence was again felt upon England. Boats, of sorts, were to be had in abundance and these, rigged out of old books on sail and only ballasted by their ruined, starved engines, began to creep up and down that waterway and even out and up the coast.

The happiness of a country is directly dependent upon the business of that country. And here everyone had seven times more projects to accomplish than he could ever hope to complete in his lifetime, and there was the grand goal of making a destroyed country live again. Everyone, therefore, was happy. And there was no worry whatever about politics.

The Lieutenant sat in audience for four hours each day, his fatigue cap on the back of his head, his elbows on his battered desk and his chin cupped attentively in his hands. He seemed oblivious of the fact that he was against a background used by half the kings of England. He would listen to a young farmer's rambling account of how things were going up in Norfolk without any indication of the fact that agriculture bored him to the point of fainting. And he would sift out the problems and solve them without much effort, and the farmer would go away happy and content that the government, for once, was in the hands of the grandest fellow alive.

To the Lieutenant would come a woman who

claimed she had been hardly used by the sergeant-major court of her district, in that the sergeant major would not compel her husband to take her best friend also to wife despite the fact that there was too much work for just one and that her friend was not needed in her present home. The Lieutenant would listen to the husband's protest that he doubted he could handle *two* women when he could barely manage one's uncertainties. And the Lieutenant, smiling, might say, like as not: "Snyder, I regret to say the deed is done. You have just been married to a second wife. Make a note of that, Mawkey." And Mawkey would grin and write it all in a book, and the farmer, now that the thing was done, determined to be cheerful about it if the Lieutenant thought it was right.

Only two things found the Lieutenant swift and savage in his action. The reiteration by some person that the B.C.P. had assigned him such and such or had decreed thus and so. Having discovered that the B.C.P., like all such governments, had manhandled affairs for the benefit of a few yes-men, the population was usually reduced by one before the hour was out. The other was discourtesy to a soldier who had served on the Continent.

In the early part of his first winter, the Lieutenant had sent Bulger and Weasel with a small command across the channel with written invitations to all field officers to return speedily with their commands. Bulger and Weasel had spent three months on the task, traveling at lightning speed and shortening their work by making every command contacted a party to the message's circulation. By the following spring most of the B.E.F. had come back. A few, of course, had founded their own spheres in Europe and would not give them up, but these were very rare, for almost all the officers and men wished to return home and hailed the Lieutenant as a savior for having accomplished the feat.

Bringing many additional nationalities with them, the B.E.F. returned. From Archangel, Syria, Spain, Poland, Estonia and Turkey, all summer the detachments continued to arrive. They numbered, in all, nearly seven thousand men and one hundred and ninety-four officers.

The process of elimination which had gone on for nearly thirty years had been very harsh but very thorough. No man without knowledge of men had lived. No officer unfit to command had continued to command. Death had been the ultimate reward for foolishness in any direction. Thus they were an iron crew, those officers, able to gauge any situation by its true values and with neither attention nor patience for any slightest attempts to swerve from the issue. The troops alone might have been said to have suffered by the exodus from Europe. For they were not overly clever at construction, schooled only in destruction, and though nearly all of them were assimilated by the National Police, saving those few kept about the officers as guards of honor, the men were very morose for a while at the prospect of inaction.

Soon, however, the spirit of construction came to them and they saw what had to be done and helped do it. In view of what the Lieutenant had done at G.H.Q. and to the B.C.P., thus avenging all of them, they were anxious to please him, the more so when they came to know him. Ruthlessly they suppressed the brigandism which had arisen in the back countries. Zealously they expedited commerce. And, which was a strange paradox, they were utterly merciless with thieves.

The officers were given great grants of land for themselves and wide districts to administer—and for this there were few enough of them. They did not abuse their rights and powers because there was no reason. Not ten followers could have been found in all the land for a project which involved removing the Lieutenant. Hence, an aristocracy was founded on the basis of skill and leadership. And it was very far from a fascism, for money and military were not combined. There was no money as such beyond the food currency. And making money for its own sake has always been a thing which a real soldier finds hard to understand. Additionally, there was no need for indirect and cunning controls over the populace. The leaders were there walking among their people, serving more than they were served. In such a way were the first nobilities of antiquity founded.

The agricultural problems which arose from the infestation of the land with insects had solved itself. Certain plants, like the few remaining people, were impervious to the insects and only these were planted. This had been started three or four years before the Lieutenant had come and by now it was arriving at a goal of extinction of plant pests.

Thus, there was plenty of food and warmth and work for all, and the country settled down into cheerful activity, forgetting its wounds and its hates. For who, with a full body, can talk earnestly of revolt and sedition? Hogarthy's corpse had been borne on the tide to the sea. The Continent was licking its wounds and wanted only to be left alone. The King of Scotland was quick to send gifts when Hanley had taken the surviving soldier Scots home with their tales of the Lieutenant.

For years affairs progressed in even tenor and then, one day, a boat was reported off Sheerness by the government at Blinker Towers.

The Lieutenant was in audience with a major from up Hereford way and was so deeply engrossed that he did not immediately hear what Weasel said. Weasel, at the risk of being insistent, repeated it and popped his heels together to demand attention.

"Sir, there's a boat. A motor vessel. It come into

the estuary about twenty minutes ago off Sheerness and dropped its hook."

"Well?" said the Lieutenant.

"A boat, sir. A big one. Big as these wrecks in the river and bigger. And it runs by engines just like our tanks used to in the old days."

The Lieutenant dismissed the major with a motion of his hand. "Any report on its flag?"

"Yessir," said Weasel, mollified now that he had his officer's attention. "It's got horizontal bars, red and white, according to the message, and a field up in the corner with a bunch of white stars."

The Lieutenant looked at the window in thought. "I can't remember any such flag. And we've no books on it, either. Weasel, run down to the barracks and see if any of the troops there know of it."

"Yessir. You think it's bad, sir?"

"How do I know? Be quick."

The Lieutenant sat down at his desk and stared unseeing at the documents there which awaited his signature. He had a chilly premonition like that time they had stormed the fortresses outside Berlin, when only himself and his colonel had come back with less than five hundred men out of six thousand. He shivered. Strange it was to feel this way, to remember suddenly that a man had nerves. He picked up his pen and then laid it down. It couldn't be cold in here, not with the mid-August sun beating down outside.

Weasel came back. "Old Chipper knows it, sir. He says he saw it once on an American vessel in Bordeaux just after the war began. He says he was just a kid, but he said the flag was so pretty he couldn't help remembering."

"And what nation is it?"

"The Union States, sir. I never heard of it myself."

"Union States?" The Lieutenant stood up and took another turn around the room. "He means the United States of America. I recall studying the tactics of Robert E. Lee at Rugby when he was fighting that country. The United States of America—the country that started the atom bombing—"

He sat down at his desk and dismissed Weasel and then, alone in that frowning old throne room, he tried to think clearly. It was a strange thing not to be able to. There was some sort of conflict in his mind that he could not disentangle. He reached for his solitaire deck and dealt out a hand. But he did not play it.

Every part of his being told him that he had to act swiftly. But he was a soldier and, as a soldier, he primarily thought of repulsing an invasion. And now, having become, perforce, a statesman, he knew that there was a chance that this ship merely wanted to establish trade like that he had with Scotland.

Because of his own victory on the Thames, he knew well how weak it was. He had caused several guns to be laboriously repaired and a few hundred heavy shells to be literally carved out of metal dug up from old bombardments. Nothing could come up the Thames unless he passed the word. Why this spirit of war which mounted so steadily in him?

Weasel came in. "Sir, another message. I just picked it off the Wapping relay tower. The vessel is landing a small party at Sheerness in a boat which is also driven by motor and very swiftly. Fast as plane, the message said, sir."

"Keep me informed," said the Lieutenant.

He sat where he was, not touching the food Mawkey brought at tea time.

Weasel came down from the upper battlement. He had a written message this time, handed him by the girl who was on duty there, for Weasel could not write, even though he could read the Gravesend Tower before Wapping could get it down.

> To the Lieutenant.
> From Commanding Officer Sheerness
>   Battery,
> Via Blinker, helio.

> U.S.S. *New York* anchored this afternoon and landed captain of vessel and twenty marines and three civilians. States pacific intentions. Wishes permission of interview with the Lieutenant.

He read the message through twice. He could find no reason to refuse such a request, though he knew that he should. But would it do any harm to talk to them?

"Send word that permission is granted," said the Lieutenant. "Wait. Send word to Swinburne, wherever he is, that he's needed here. And wait again, Weasel. Have the adjutant issue Order A."

Weasel was startled, not to have Order A issued, which was the manning of all guns and garrisons, but to hear a note of tired kindness in the Lieutenant's voice. Another might not have detected it. But Weasel, who had seen many officers face defeat and death, recognized it for what it was. He stayed for a little longer and then, unwillingly, turned and went out.

The Lieutenant dealt another hand of solitaire, but he did not play it. Bugles began to blare about the keep. Commands barked. He wandered to the window and, half sitting on the ledge, looked down at the Inner Ward.

Troops were hurrying out, dragging their equipment after them and getting into it as they jolted each other, straightening out their lines. These were infantry scouts whose positions lay about the base of Tower Hill. A company of snipers was hurrying from their quarters in the Bloody Tower to man the battlements of the outer wall, hands full of bandoleers and spare rifles. Gian was checking his men as they leaped by him and up the steps to their guns on the twelve towers of the Inner Wall.

Mounted messengers were saddling skittish Scot horses, holding their orders in their teeth and swearing as only couriers can swear. Bit by bit these streamed out of the Inner Ward and thundered through the Byward Tower and across the moat to be swallowed from sight by the stone houses which circled the base of the hill.

The scout company of the Fourth Brigade, to which was entrusted the defense of the pièce de résistance, the White Tower where the Lieutenant had his quarters and offices in company with the ghosts of England's monarchs, followed hard on the heels of Carstair up the steps.

The hot August sun slanted its rays upon the swirling cloaks and helmets—brightened in peace— of officers who came up from the town to be detailed by Carstair on special duty.

The Lieutenant raised his eyes from the gray walls and blue uniforms below and looked at the banner which floated lazily from its staff upon the Byward Tower, over the gate. Satiny white it was, with the insignia of a lieutenant embroidered upon it in gold. It had been presented to him by the people and, to them, represented peace and security and justice. To him it represented the confidence reposed in him by his people, not unlike that which he had received from the Fourth Brigade. No questions were asked or had ever been asked by his soldiers or his people.

From his vantage point he could see far down

the Thames and he looked in that direction now. The river was spotted with traffic, ships from his coasts, sailing up to London, barges plying across the stream or bringing produce down from the upper reaches, small skiffs filled with pleasure seekers. But these, as bugles resounded at the batteries, were now making for shore, leaving the river a great yellow expanse, hot in the sunlight.

Weasel came in. "Everything is ready, sir. I took it for granted you did not want to be bothered with reports."

"Thank you, Weasel."

"Sir—"

But whatever Weasel said was engulfed in a roar of sound. The Lieutenant instinctively moved back from the window and Weasel threw himself down flat on the pave. But no following scream resulted, no machine guns chattered and, in a moment, Weasel picked himself up. His gesture was so thoroughly a part of training ingrained by the years that he did not even remark upon it. Curiously he advanced to the window beside the Lieutenant.

Mawkey hurled himself into the room and stood there, big-eyed and hunched up. "A plane just went over!"

The snarl resounded again and Mawkey pushed himself flat against the wall and tensed. The ship took two turns above London and then vanished so swiftly to the east that it appeared to have shrunken suddenly to nothing.

"Reconnaissance," said Weasel. "I haven't seen one of those for years!"

Carstair came in from above. "Sir, Gian signaled me to ask if you want to shoot the next time it comes over."

"With what?" said the Lieutenant.

Carstair stood a little straighter. "Yes, that's so. I've never seen anything so fast. All motors and guns and bombs."

The Lieutenant did not turn from the window. "Pass the word if anyone wants to leave this fortress, he has my permission."

"I can answer that now," said Carstair. "When we leave it will be over the wall into the river—dead."

The Lieutenant did not speak.

Carstair beckoned and Weasel and Mawkey slid out, closing the doors behind them. The Lieutenant hardly knew they were gone. Suddenly he turned around and marched to his desk. He picked up his cards and then hurled them to the floor. He went back to the window.

In a few minutes he saw the sun glance off metal far downriver. And even as he looked the boat grew in size. It hurled back very little spray, but it scudded upstream like some possessed water bug. It went into reverse and shot sideways to the Queen's Steps at the Tower wharf and out of it leaped a guard of marines, resplendent in blue.

The Lieutenant could not see what passed, but, in a moment, Carstair came in. "Sir, they are armed, each man with a sort of miniature machine gun. Your orders?"

"Is Swinburne here?"

"He came a moment ago."

"Send him up. And let them come in immediately after. I'll appreciate it if you and any other officers who happen to be here will step in for the reception."

"Let them in armed?"

"Why not?"

"Yes, sir." Carstair went away.

Presently Swinburne came up the steps. He was just back from a long trip inland, inspecting some of the new homes of the countryside, and he was still lathered by his horse and his boots were muddy. But his one good eye blazed and his empty sleeve was thrust angrily into his tunic pocket.

"What's this, old fellow?"

"United States of America. A battleship standing off Sheerness. Its captain and some civilians coming up for an interview."

Swinburne scowled and laid his crop and cap upon the window seat. "Anything I can do?"

"Just stand by."

Carstair stepped in. "Everyone else at his post along the river."

"All right. Show them up."

Swinburne was sensible of a stiffening in the

Lieutenant's bearing as he sat down in the great chair. Swinburne stood on his right, hand on the chair back.

A double file of soldiers could be heard taking positions on the landing, to their side of the door, and then Carstair opened it and, standing at attention, said, "Three Americans to see you, sir."

"Let them come in," said Swinburne.

Carstair stepped back on the inside. A glint of polished metal gleamed where the marines stood at the top of the steps. The three Americans marched between the honor-guard files and into the room. Carstair closed the door and stood with back against it, arms folded. Probably he was the only man in the garrison who knew the United States from actual contact, for he had crossed it on his way to England fourteen years before.

The two gentlemen in the lead were dressed in somber clothing of a loose cut which gave their rotund figures even more breadth. They were both rather soft-looking, for their jowls were loose and their stomachs protruded. One was clearly a dynamic fellow, whose head was bushy with gray hair and whose eyes held a piercing look which was almost a challenge. He was the leader.

"I," he said with unction, "am Senator Frisman of Arkansas. This is my brother in diplomacy, Senator Breckwell, Jefferson Breckwell, who represents the proud State of Ohio in our nation's capital at

Washington. And while we are party enemies, he being a Socialist and myself a Social-Democrat, we are firm friends. May I present Senator Breckwell?"

Breckwell bowed. He was a rather vacant-faced fellow, completely bald, having a pair of very mild and apologetic eyes which dropped the instant they met the Lieutenant's.

Senator Frisman cleared his throat. "And may I also present that very able captain of our nation's powerful fleet, who commands one of our finest cruisers as well as our admiring respect, Captain Johnson."

Stealing an uneasy glance at Senator Frisman, Captain Johnson bowed. He was a gaunt, hard fellow who smacked of the sea and the bridge. He did not approve of Senator Frisman.

"And so," said Frisman, unaware of the silence which was greeting his loquacity, "we are proud to be able to meet your majesty, for we have excellent news for our English brothers."

Swinburne's voice had always had the quality of a sputtering fuse, but now it sizzled. "You are addressing the Lieutenant, gentlemen. He has been good enough to grant you audience. Please come to the point."

"The Lieutenant?" said Frisman. "But we have nothing to do with your army. We wish to speak to your dictator or king or Communist leader—"

" 'The Lieutenant' is a title," said Swinburne. "He rules here."

"But," said Frisman, "a lieutenant is just a lower rank in the army and we—"

"The title," said Swinburne, keeping his patience, "has been removed from our army list out of respect. You said something about a message."

Frisman realized suddenly that he wasn't doing so well. Captain Johnson was glaring at him and even Senator Breckwell was fumbling with his collar. They had suddenly become acutely aware of the Lieutenant.

He sat quite still. Altogether too still. His eyes were calm, as though masking a great deal, a fact which was far more effective than an outright glare. He was slender and hard and good-looking, having yet to celebrate his thirty-second birthday. His tunic was blue, faded but well pressed and clean, innocent of any bright work other than the simple insignia of his rank. He wore, as a habit too old to break, crossbelts of dull leather, to which was holstered an automatic pistol. His small blue fatigue cap sat a little over one ear, but his helmet, with visor raised, was close by upon his desk. His cape, patched where a hundred and more bullets had struck, lay over the back of his chair. He did not feel comfortable without these things at his hand, for they had been part of him too long. A shaft of late-afternoon sun came like a beam through the upper windows and lay in a pool upon the desk before him, rendering the Lieutenant all the more indefinite of image behind it.

• • •

The antiquity of this place with its thick, scarred walls began to enter into the trio. They were sensible that here was England, whether in the garb of a soldier or in the gaudy robes of a king.

"Captain Johnson," said the Lieutenant, "will you please step here to the desk and be seated?"

Johnson was made uneasy by the order for it was an affront to the two civilians. But civilians, to the Lieutenant, were either politicians or peasants, both equally bad.

Johnson eased himself into the chair. He was a competent officer and an excellent judge of men and he had some idea now of whom he faced.

"Captain Johnson," said the Lieutenant, "a little while ago a battle plane flew over London. That, I presume, was from your ship?"

"Yes," said Johnson. "We wished to make sure that the river was clear."

"And yet it might have dropped bombs."

"I am sorry if it has offended."

"I do not recall giving any permission other than that you might call here."

"I offer my apologies."

"You have not been at war for many, many years," said the Lieutenant. "At least, so far as I know. You have not seen bombers wipe out whole cities and populations. The presence of that ship in our skies, in other times, would have been construed as a declaration of war. Unfortunately we had no antiaircraft batteries or we would have shot it down without orders, thus creating a very bad incident."

"If I had known—"

"That flight and the pictures you probably took of the countryside and our batteries downriver have told you how poor are our defenses. Against that one plane we are helpless."

Captain Johnson colored a little with shame. There had been pictures. "I shall turn them over to you. Call in the guard and I shall bring you the strips."

"That will do no good. You have already seen them. Very well. Let us forget it. Will you please acquaint me with the purpose of this visit?"

Johnson hesitated, glancing at Frisman. The senator and his confrere accepted it as an order and stepped closer to the desk, ranging beside Johnson.

"We have come on a mission of mercy," said Frisman. "We know how desolate your nation has been made by war—"

"Why didn't you come years ago?"

"The disease known as soldier's sickness put a stop to all transatlantic traffic. And then the insect plagues—"

"Why aren't you afraid of these now?" said the Lieutenant.

"Because we have succeeded in perfecting serums and poisons to combat the scourges. We have," he said eagerly, "a great quantity of this serum aboard and if you like—"

"One was developed here. Out of human blood. And we need no serum for we are naturally immune. And we need no plant-insect poison for we have crops which withstand them."

"But food—" began Frisman. It was the start of something dramatic, but it was cut off.

"We raise all the food and supplies which we can use."

Frisman sagged a little. He felt like a man beating against stone. "Your—I mean, Lieutenant. It has been long since that cry, 'Hands Across the Sea,' was sounded. But now, at last, it can be cried out once more. We wish to do anything we can to rehabilitate your country. We can have shiploads of machinery and skilled workmen, planes, trains, and steamers which we can give you. Our only wish is to see this country blossom. And we mean to say not a word about debts, considering that the surrender of British colonies in the Americas has evened the score completely. We are even prepared to restore this nation to its once proud state, giving it back its African possessions and all the development which has been done upon them. Your land cries out for succor. We are back to the birthplace of our own proud nation, offering to repay the debt of centuries—"

"Who is this man?" said the Lieutenant to Johnson.

The naval officer looked uncomfortable. "He is a great man in our country, the leader of the majority group of the Senate and chairman of the Foreign Affairs and Colonies Committee."

"Committee?" said the Lieutenant, for the word had taken on poison from the B.C.P.

"Yes," beamed Frisman. "And my worthy friend, Senator Breckwell of Ohio, is the leading light of the second great party of the United States, the Socialist Party."

England's Socialist leader had led an abortive revolt, starting it with the assassination of many members of Parliament. The leader, on trial, had gone free by giving up his lists and was later shot as a traitor by his own people. The Lieutenant gave Jefferson Breckwell a very perfunctory glance. He had no respect for creeds or statesmen: between the two the Continent and the British Isles had been destroyed. Thirty million fighting men and three hundred million civilians had paid with their lives for mistaken faith in creeds and statesmen.

The Lieutenant turned to the naval officer. Here he had someone with whom he could talk, that he could anticipate, and, as one military leader to another, trust.

"We do not need these things," said the Lieutenant. "We have almost doubled our population in two years and we have the situation in hand. We have food and we are happy. Machines only make unemployment and, ultimately, politicians out of otherwise sensible men. Understand me, Captain Johnson, for I speak true. We thank you for your aid, but we do not need it. An influx of food and machines would disrupt this country no less than a horde of strangers. We have found that it is better to build than to destroy, for in building there is occupation for the body and the mind. When each man does his best with his materials at hand, he is proud of his work and is happy with his life. Hatred only rises when some agency destroys or attempts to destroy those things of which we are the most proud—our crafts, our traditions, our faith in man.

"Captain Johnson, I have always been a soldier. Until a few years ago I was continually surrounded by war; I did not know that such a thing as peace existed. I saw great, intricate fabrics of nations come tearing down to dust and rubble and death; hatred was the cause of this, a hatred bred by politicians against politicians, creeds battling senseless creeds. In the last years I have found what peace could mean and I am not anxious for war."

"We do not come speaking of war," said Johnson, aghast.

"The first step in any war is the landing of armed forces. A plane overhead, marines out there on the landing, a cruiser off Sheerness—"

"Sir," cried Frisman, "the United States of America is a peace-loving nation. We withdrew from the second phase of World War II because we were atomic bombed, and sensibly refrained from re-entering even when we had completely rebuilt because we well knew that we alone would be the well of civilization when all here was destroyed. And now we mean to rescue an exhausted people and restore the bright light of culture—"

"Captain Johnson," said the Lieutenant, "at one time this nation was densely overpopulated. The weak and stupid were supported by the king with a dole. We shipped in great quantities of raw materials and manufactured them. We shipped in our food or starved. But this land is fertile and this nation can support itself. Empire was a mirage. With it this land was involved in war. With it this land starved. We have lost all our weaklings now. We are seven hundred and fifty thousand people, and not until almost a century has sped will we begin to take up the available land. Perhaps then we will go all through the cycle once more. But just now we see ahead a century of plenty and therefore a century of internal peace. Then, perhaps, war will come again. But it will not come until we again have so little that people will be foolish enough to listen to the harpings of political mob makers. A new influx of population now will restore that chaotic stupidity which your civilian friend here calls 'culture.' The only good government is that government under which a people is busy and, as an individual, is valued for himself. Such a government exists. We want no machines, no colonizers, no foreign 'culture.' We are not an exhausted people, but a small, compact band that was strong enough to survive bullets and bombs, starvation and disease.

"I am neither a politician nor a statesman; I am a soldier. I know nothing of the chicanery which goes by the name of diplomacy. But I learned long ago that there is only one way to rule, and that is for the good of all; that the function of a commanding officer of a company or a state is to protect the rights of the individual within the bounds of common good, but never to trifle with the actual welfare of any man or to attempt to carry any man beyond his own ability and strength, for to do so weakens the position of all and is not for the common good. A state, gentlemen, is not a charity institution. On this score alone I cannot accept your gifts. Now, if you please, the interview is ended. I shall be pleased to receive a report from my Sheerness Battery commander tomorrow morning that the horizon is empty."

Swinburne had never heard the Lieutenant speak before, had never believed that he could. But now he knew that the Lieutenant had pleaded for the life of the country he had returned from the dead—and it seemed that he had won.

Yes, it seemed that he had won. Captain Johnson stood up. Frisman glared, but was too baffled to find anything to say. Breckwell grinned a foolish and bewildered grin. This boy in faded blue, backed by his battle cape and flanked by his helmet, had made no move toward them. He had anticipated their desires, had fully outlined, by inference, their plans. He had left them nothing whatever to advance, for any effort to compel him would be to accept the low valuations he had put upon such motives. In the face of what he had said, the only decent thing to do would be to leave England strictly alone.

Frisman writhed. He had a high opinion of his own diplomatic talents and of his silver tongue. And yet, here was a soldier, actually a junior officer of some sort, completely outmaneuvering him. Every method of advance had been stopped, completely and thoroughly. They could not attack, for he had told them that the place was defenseless against them. They could not buy him, because he said that food and machinery would ruin his country. They could not colonize the place, because, guilelessly, he had made that into the form of a national insult. He had not threatened or argued, for they had been able to advance only a small portion of their desires before he had grasped them all and had thrown them back in their faces.

Frisman almost heeded Captain Johnson's tugging hand. But then, before Frisman arose the figure of himself in the United States Senate, pleading with tears in his voice to succor the starving women and children of Europe, begging an appropriation for the cause and not once mentioning the possibilities of colonization, for the press had been extremely trying of late on the subject of the new-reborn imperialistic aims of the Social-Democratic regime. And Frisman saw himself going back, his succor refused, his appropriation unspent and himself the butt of the minority jokes. Suddenly it came over him that he had been trussed up in a snare of words, that it did not matter what he said, backed up as he was by a cruiser. But still—the strange quietness of this officer— No. No, he could not threaten. He did not know if Johnson would back him—

Before him rose up the images of all those millions and millions of idle workers who had boosted him to where he was on the promise that he would give them the wide horizons to redeem, in place of those huge areas of radioactive prohibited land. This country alone would take twenty million of them. And what projects for an industrial state! To rebuild— To restore the nation which had given birth to the United States— How his name would thunder down the pages of history!

He had had a plan. All this had evolved from one incident. America had gotten along so well for so long without Europe that public sentiment had been against any future interference whatever until—

Johnson was beckoning, having already gotten Breckwell to the door which Carstair held open. Frisman felt that the pause was awkward, but he knew that if he left this room, the whole project was at an end and his promises and pleas were all empty.

"Lieutenant," said Frisman, stepping up to the

desk again, "there is one fact with which I feel I should acquaint you for your own peace of mind."

The Lieutenant did not speak.

"This spring," said Frisman, "there arrived on our Florida coast a Spanish fishing vessel. It held a very strange crew and stranger passengers. And the tales which were told by these passengers of the rapacity of the present English government stirred our populace until something had to be done. We heard of the wanton murder of your last Communist ruler, of soldiers pillaging and burning all that was left of England, of children starving and women despoiled. This cruel aftermath of a devastating war was more than our people could permit. They demanded that something be done. The passengers of that fishing vessel are aboard the U.S.S. *New York*, off Sheerness. What shall I tell them?"

As Frisman had spoken, the Lieutenant had tensed. He came suddenly to his feet now, white of visage and harsh of voice. "Who are these liars?"

"The heads of the British army in France," said Frisman. "General Victor and his adjutant, Colonel Smythe."

Swinburne had swiftly capped the Lieutenant's holster flap. Frisman completely missed the byplay.

"We cannot allow," said Frisman, "a continuance of such affairs. Our people would denounce us. As the chosen representative of a powerful government I must demand that a place be made for these two fficers so that they can be certain their land will ot be completely shattered. And you cannot help ut accede to this, for they are, in the final analysis, our own superiors."

Swinburne spoke. "You seem to forget that you peak to the ruler of England. Such demands are no ess insulting than your accusations. He has bidden ou to leave. Do so."

But Senator Frisman had seen his advantage. "I annot understand any reason why you should not onor your own superiors if your rule here is as ighteous as you claim. Freedom of person is the test f such a rule. It is our purpose to repatriate these nen and give them their just share in this country's ffairs."

Swinburne had the holster flap securely closed nd kept it that way.

The Lieutenant steadied. "Your proposal is ery plain. Unable to do business with us, you are repared to install, by force if necessary, a govern- nent which will let you have your way here."

"Rather crudely stated," said Frisman, "but per- aps it is near the truth. We cannot allow a popu- ce to be abused—"

"Please don't attempt a cloak of humanitarian- m," said the Lieutenant. "It becomes you very adly. You want this land. Your nation is overpopu- ted today as ours was many years ago. Perhaps nuch of your land is spoiled? You need England to ase that burden."

189

The Lieutenant's voice was almost monotonous, and Frisman, feeling a decided gain, lost h
earlier respect for this fellow. "If you wish to s
state it."

"In the event that this nation was to honor you
requests, would you be prepared to give those peo
ple still alive here every benefit and liberty?"

"I should say so."

"And you would be prepared to deliver up to u
this General Victor and Colonel Smythe?"

Frisman smiled and shook his head. "So that :
the direction in which this leads? It is wholly impos
sible. Do you consider us traitors?"

"You have all the force," said the Lieutenan
"It is not for me to bargain." He sat down and, fo
a little while, somberly regarded his helmet. "Ver
well. Bring those two men here and what docu
ments you might have concerning any treaty, an
tonight we shall arrange matters."

"You definitely agree?"

"I agree to make Colonel Smythe and Genera
Victor the supreme heads of the English goverr
ment." And he forestalled Frisman by adding
"Now you may go."

Frisman, beaming, went. Just before the doc
was closed he looked back. The beam of light fror
the high window was gone now. The Lieutenant sa
very still in the murky gloom of the ancient room
eyes cast down.

Chapter X

Swinburne was too amazed to find anything to say at first. He wandered about the room with agitated steps, pausing now and then to stare through the window at the darkening river. Finally he came back to the desk, having seen the gig depart.

"Lieutenant, I cannot understand this. To surrender without any battle to a power which will wipe out everything which was ever England—"

"A power," said Carstair by the door, "which is the greatest on earth now."

"That may be," said Swinburne, "but England is England. And to give up everything for which we have worked these past years, to be swallowed up in a beehive of humanity from alien shores—I can't support these things."

"The United States could wipe us out completely," said Carstair.

"Better to be wiped out in a blood bath than to quit like cowards," growled Swinburne. "They came here to put Victor at the head of the govern- ment so that he would do their bidding. Victor! He sold out a dictator that placed all his trust in him! He was too slippery a turncoat to be kept even by *Hogarthy!* He bungled everything he ever did in France and cost Heaven knows how many millions of lives! And, having betrayed his army to set up his own regime, he now goes whining to the United States in the guise of a monarchist! And you," he cried, suddenly angry and facing the Lieutenant, "are agreeable to putting him in your place!"

Mawkey slipped in, his quick eyes not missing anything that went on. "Sir, Captain Thorbridge from Sheerness is here."

The Lieutenant motioned that he be admitted.

Thorbridge was a tall youth who spoke habit- ually in a staccato voice. He took his duties of ship inspector at Sheerness very seriously.

"Sir, I've ridden hell out of a horse. Inspected the U.S.S. *New York*. They didn't seem to care what I saw. I came up here as quick as I could. Gad, what a ship!

"Sir, she's nearly six hundred feet long. She's got engines they claim drive her at eighty knots. She's like a torpedo and nothing's exposed on her at all. There's a couple hatches they let planes out of and by Heaven, sir, those planes can land right back. The Hay's Heliplane, they're called. Rotoprops, no wings, go straight up at four hundred, straight ahead at six hundred and fifty.

"Sir, you ought to see her armament. She hasn't a gun aboard! Every projectile is its own gun like those rocket shells we saw about ten years ago at the front, only these really work. They're like rocket planes and they go up out of chutes and they fire at any range up to a thousand miles. Got away from gun barrels and danger of explosion and all that. They claim one of those shells could wipe out any ship and a half a dozen any city.

"Sir, she steers herself and runs herself and submerges if necessary, and by Heaven the only thing she won't do is fly. And they claim nothing except her own armament can make a dent in her!

"I came right up. If she was to cut loose on us there wouldn't be a damned thing left, sir. Not a damn thing!"

"Thank you," said the Lieutenant, dully.

Thorbridge withdrew with the feeling that something was very wrong with the Lieutenant. He would have been convinced could he have seen what happened after.

The Lieutenant slumped more deeply into the great chair. "You see, gentlemen?"

Swinburne paced about. "But, confound it, there might be some way of making concessions without putting Victor and Smythe at the head of everything! Man, don't you know what they'll do? They'll revive all the creeds and claptrap that we once had.

They'll ape their masters and throw our people into the nearest ditch!"

"As long as the ship out there is convinced that this must be done," said the Lieutenant, "it must be done. They refused to give us Victor and Smythe for execution which they justly deserve. They'll treat fairly that way, anyhow."

"Fairly! They're afraid to leave you here!" snapped Swinburne. And then he considered what he had just said and came back to the desk. "The first duty of any officer is to his command, Lieutenant. This nation is just as much your command as your brigade ever was. I've never heard it said that you neglected that brigade. And yet you can conceive of allowing us to fall into the hands of two renegade tools of a powerful and voracious—"

"You talk like that Frisman," said the Lieutenant tiredly. He sat a little straighter then. "I've never neglected my command. To do other than grant the wishes of these people would be to wipe out England completely. They ask only for an incident to take us over for a colony. Can't you see that. Only if our government here behaves perfectly can we stave off becoming part of another nation. So long as we can prove ourselves to be acting in the best interests of everyone, there will be no excuse whatever for them to assimilate us. We *must* see that this government acts in good faith, that it is fairly conducted for all, that no incident will occur which will permit them to establish martial rule here

Please," he said, slumping back, "please remember what I have said."

Swinburne was plainly disgusted. "A thief comes up and sticks a gun in your ribs and so, rather than risk getting hurt, you tamely say: 'Yes, here is my wallet. And my wives and goods at home are at your complete disposal.' You call *that* statesmanship!"

"He can do nothing else," said Carstair.

"Bah!" said Swinburne. "These years of peace have turned him into putty!" And he stalked from the room, slamming the door behind him.

"Carstair," said the Lieutenant, "he is going out to call a council of officers. Please make sure that you give them my orders. I am to have this evening. They will have all the tomorrows. Tell them that upon the return of the people, they must come in here and stand as witness to what takes place and to pledge their faith to Victor and Smythe so long as they may rule."

"But they won't!" cried Carstair. "We are field officers!"

"Nevertheless, ask them to have faith and do what I say. It is for the best. Have I ever given a foolish order before, good friend?"

Carstair hesitated and his memory shot back over the past to the time he had first seen this man at G.H.Q. "No. No, you have never given a foolish order."

"Then tell them to save their revolts for the

morrow and to let me have tonight. They must come in and agree—that is necessary, Carstair."

"They'll accuse you of cowardice."

"Let them."

"Can't you see that the first official act of Victor will be the ordering of your execution?" begged Carstair. "As soon as those Americans have left, Victor will rake up followers from the rabble and Heaven knows what things will happen. And we won't be able to touch him. They'll leave a large guard with him, that's a certainty. Did you see the arms of those marines? Why, that twenty, with those small automatic weapons and those bulletproof jackets and their pocket radios—"

"I care nothing about these things; I am only thinking of my command—for when the command is destroyed the officer also dies. But, one way or another, an officer lives so long as his command lives. Go now, Carstair, and tell them what I say."

There was something in the Lieutenant's tone which made Carstair fear for him; but the Australian said no more. Quietly he closed the door behind him.

Sometime later Mawkey slipped in, looking smaller and more twisted than usual and his eyes dull. He carried a tray for an excuse and stood by while the Lieutenant minced at the food.

"Sir," ventured Mawkey, "is it true that you are going to let General Victor become the ruler here?"

The Lieutenant nodded wearily.

"If you say so, sir, then it's so. But me and

Bulger and Pollard and Weasel and Carstone have been talking. We got it figured out that the way you made a rabbit out of that Victor, the first thing he'll do will be to kill you. Now, if we was to shoot this Victor and this Smythe soon as they got inside the Tower—"

"Those marines would murder the lot of you."

"Yessir. But that's better than letting Victor execute the Lieutenant."

"Haven't you seen the guns those marines carry?"

"Sure. They could tear a man in half and nothing we've got could stop those slugs. But we ain't afraid of no marines, sir. It's the man, that's what counts."

"Mawkey, you'll do as I tell you. As soon as we get the proper documents signed in here, every one of my soldiers and officers is to leave Tower Hill."

"What's that, sir?"

"And stay away."

"And you, sir?"

"I'll stay here."

Mawkey was troubled, but he knew no other way to counter this. It was plain to him that the Lieutenant had suddenly developed a suicidal mania like so many other officers had in the face of defeat.

"Remember my orders," said the Lieutenant when Mawkey had picked up the tray.

"Yessir," said Mawkey, but with difficulty for there was something wrong with his throat and his eyes smarted.

• • •

Promptly at eight, the gig slowed to a stop at the Queen's Steps and made fast her lines. The party was as before with the addition of two more members. And the Tower was as before with the exception that its guards glared with sullen mien upon the intruders.

The files of marines felt the heaviness of the atmosphere and tried to put their boots down quietly upon the pave to still the echoes of the ancient, gray battlements. They were experienced soldiers, those marines, with the high-tuned senses of the fighting man, for they had served with Clayton in Mexico, taking all the shock work so the army could grab the glory. They had wiped out the last fortress in the Yellow Sea; they had chased down the last mad dictator in Central America. In ten years of service they had set the Stars and Stripes to float above all the Western Hemisphere and half of Asia. And they knew the feel of hostility held off with effort. But, aside from their soldier-sailor selves and their professional duties, they were not at ease about this thing, for they saw the antiquated rifles and field guns in the ranks of the guard and it jibed strangely with these faces so like their own. It was as if some of themselves had suddenly been transplanted to an enemy—and they had never fought their own race before.

But if the marines were still and if their young officer was alert as a cat, none of this reached

Frisman and his companions. Captain Johnson had seen fit to stay aboard, for he had no stomach for this, and Frisman was relieved about it, never having liked anything which smacked of military etiquette and stiffness.

Colonel Smythe and Frisman kept up a brisk stream of self-congratulatory conversation. They were much of a kind, though the senator looked like a lion beside this jackal. General Victor's large, lolling head was bobbing erectly as he tried to make himself look as much like a conqueror as possible. Even Breckwell discovered self-importance and managed to get some of it into his usually empty face.

They were passed through the gates and the Inner Ward and into the Norman keep. As they mounted the steps they began to get themselves in order, the marines looking closely to the fighting characteristics of the place and Frisman clearing his throat and thinking up some resounding trite phrases.

About thirty men of the old Fourth Brigade were drawn about the entrance to the great hall, and among them were Bulger, Pollard, Weasel, Tou-tou, old Chipper, Gian and Mawkey, a rather large number of high-ranking noncoms for so small a group. They stood as though they were permanent fixtures of the grim, old place.

Carstair stood at the door and watched them arrive without giving any sign that he saw them at all. But when they were all there he turned and stepped in.

"They have arrived, sir."

"Let them come in."

Frisman pushed forward. He had little eye for detail, but even to him things had changed. The room was somberly lit by two candelabra and a girandole, but the candles did no more than intensify the darkness of the lofty ceiling and the shadows on the walls.

The lieutenant sat at his desk, robed in his battle cloak, helmet before him. All the contents of the files were tied into bundles on the floor and what few possessions he had were laid out beside them.

Along the wall was a stony frieze of officers who gave Frisman a glance and then bent a harsh regard upon Victor and Smythe.

Victor lost a little of his certainty. His wabbly head bobbed as he scanned the line. He recognized them one by one. Field officers that he had failed to trick into turning back their commands and some that he had. Victor gave a glance to the marines outside and was instantly reassured.

"Good evening, sir," said Frisman. "And gentlemen," to the officers. "I trust that we are all of the same mind that we were this afternoon?"

The Lieutenant fingered a document before him. "I am. Shall we get through this thing as quickly as possible?"

"Certainly," said Frisman. "Here are my credentials and such, giving me power to act freely in this matter. No restraints were placed upon me by my government, as you will see."

The Lieutenant barely glanced at them. He gave Frisman a cold stare. "I have prepared the terms. To avoid any friction or complication, I have drawn up a governmental procedure. I shall withdraw completely."

Victor almost smiled.

"But," said the Lieutenant, "I have a condition to make. That you will keep my plan in operation."

"And this plan?" said Frisman.

"General Victor shall be in full and unopposed command of the country and all its defenses. In case anything happens to him, he is to be succeeded by Colonel Smythe, who will again have dictatorial powers. In case anything should happen to Smythe, the country is to be governed by its officers corps, who will recognize Swinburne as their chairman. Is this agreeable?"

"Certainly," said Frisman, not having hoped for so much.

"Further," said the Lieutenant, "I have limited immigration of Americans to England to a hundred thousand a month. These immigrants are to purchase their land from the present owners at the fair price, which shall, in no case, be less than fifteen pounds an acre at the exchange of five dollars to a pound."

"That is rather steep," said Frisman.

"For English land? Indeed, it is rather cheap," said the Lieutenant. "Do you agree?"

"In view of all else, yes."

"Then, to proceed. All titles to the land issued during my regime shall be honored. Agreed?"

"Yes."

"Now, about law enforcement. The national police shall be wholly within British control, just as the government shall be. No man shall be an officer in the army unless he is born British. Agreed?"

"You drive a stiff bargain."

"I am giving you a country. If you want it, you shall have to accept these conditions. This document of yours gives you full power to reorganize any government. That is binding, is it not?"

"Yes."

"Then you have reorganized this government no more than to accept General Victor here as its chief. All judges will remain British. Agreed?"

"Yes."

"You are to turn over to this new government adequate methods of defense. Equipment equal to that of your own troops. And in quantity to arm forty thousand men to be delivered not later than next month. Agreed?"

"Yes, of course."

"All laws as laid down by myself will continue in force. All honors conferred by me shall be respected. And if you are willing to sign this and have it witnessed, the business is done."

Frisman looked the document over. He wanted nothing better than this, for it meant that he could ease the pressure of the idle in the Americas. Very few had any liking for the new South American States. But the climate and soil of England was a definite lure. And when they had Europe, a feat for which the unemployed had been anxiously waiting, the whole thing would be solved. Yes, this document was very carefully phrased and very binding. But with Victor at the head— Frisman smiled and signed.

When the formalities were finished the Lieutenant handed the document to a sour Swinburne and turned back to address Frisman. "I am now withdrawing completely from the government of England, relinquishing all title and command. Here is a statement to that effect for your records." And he handed the paper over. "And now, if all is in order, I have one last order to give."

"Of course," said Frisman.

"Gentlemen," said the Lieutenant to his officers, "you will please carry out my last request to you. Evacuate Tower Hill with all troops so that General Victor can feel free to organize a new guard. If he wishes to call any of you, let him find you in the town."

Bitterly they filed past the Lieutenant, past the marines at the door and vanished down the steps. For some little time there was a rhythmic sound of marching and then, slowly, silence descended upon the nearly deserted Tower Hill.

The Lieutenant, having seen them go from the window, turned back to the room. His face was impassive. He picked up his helmet and put it on, his glance lingering for a moment on the weapons of the marines who had now entered the room. His next statement was very strange to them all.

"When an officer loses his command, that officer is also lost. But when that command remains, no matter what happens to its officer, he has not failed. General Victor, you are in complete command of this government. Next in line is Smythe. After that the corps of officers as a council. You all agree, I hope, that I now have nothing whatever to do with the British government?"

They nodded, a little mystified. Victor's wabbly head bobbed in complete and earnest agreement.

"I am a civilian now," said the Lieutenant, "for I even relinquish my rank, as that paper I gave you will show. The law applies wholly to me, even though I made the law. The British government, now under you, General Victor, is not at all responsible for my actions."

"True, true," said Smythe.

"Then," said the Lieutenant, standing before them all, "I shall do what I have to do."

His hand flashed from beneath the battle cloak. Flame stabbed and thundered.

Victor, half his head blown off, reeled and slumped.

Smythe tried to cover the hole in his chest with

his hands. He sought to scream, but only blood came. He tripped over Victor and thudded down, writhing.

Frisman stood in stupefied amazement, finally to lift his eyes in horror to the Lieutenant. And the thought had no more than struck home to Frisman than he flung himself back to get the protection of the marines. Breckwell began to gibber, unable to move.

The marines swept forward. Like a duelist the Lieutenant raised his arm and fired. A bullet ricocheted from the marine officer's breastplate and, instinctively, he fired at the source.

The bullet tore through the cloak as though it had been flame and the cloak paper. The Lieutenant staggered back and strove to lift his gun again.

A coughing chatter set up just outside the door. Two marines went down and the rest whirled. Carstone was there, astride the saddle of a pneumatic. The marines charged toward him, scarcely touched by the slow slugs.

Carstone's face vanished, but his fingers kept the trips down. The gun tilted up and, still firing, raked high on the wall.

Over Carstone swirled a compact knot of fighters. Tou-tou wasted no time with bullets, but used the butt of his gun. Mawkey smashed into the mass with his chain. Bulger carved a wide path with his bayonet and almost got to the Lieutenant before he staggered, gripping at his stomach, to go down.

The Lieutenant tried to shout to his men, but he could get no sound forth. In agony he watched them cut to pieces by superior weapons. Tou-tou down. Pollard, his arm gone, fighting on. A tangled thundering mass of soldiery, restricted by the walls jammed into a whirlpool of savage destruction.

Somebody was tugging at the Lieutenant's shoulders. The room began to spin from the pain of it. Again he tried to cry out and again no sound came forth.

He was falling down, down, down in a red walled pit which had a clear brilliance at the bottom. And then blackness swept away everything. Blackness and nothingness—forever.

Above the Byward Gate on Tower Hill that flag still flies; the gold is so faded that only one who knows can trace the marks which once made so clear the insignia of a lieutenant, the white field is bleached and patched where furious winds have torn it. It is the first thing men look to in the morning and the last thing men see when the sky fades out and the clear, sad notes of retreat are sounded by the British bugler on Tower Hill.

That flag still flies, and on the plaque below are graven the words:

When that command remains, no matter what happens to its officer, he has not failed.

Glossary

The numbers that appear in parentheses directly following the entry words of each definition indicate the page number where the word first appears in the text.

ack-ack: (pg. 3) *Slang.* An antiaircraft gun or its fire.—*Webster's New World Dictionary*

adjutant: (pg. 86) *Military.* A staff officer who serves as an administrative assistant to the commanding officer.
—*Webster's New World Dictionary*

batman: (pg. 91) The orderly of an officer in the British army.
—*Webster's New World Dictionary*

B.E.F.: (pg. 6) British Expeditionary Force(s): armed forces stationed outside Great Britain.—*Funk & Wagnall's Dictionary*

Belgian alcohol machine gun: (pg. 21) An automatic firearm which fires a continuous stream of bullets fed into it. It is usually mounted and has a cooling apparatus using water, air, or, in this case, alcohol.—*Webster's New World Dictionary* and Editors

billeting: (pg. 56) Lodging for soldiers in nonmilitary buildings.—*Random House Dictionary*

blockhouse: (pg. 129) *Military.* A small defensive structure of concrete.
—*Webster's New World Dictionary*

breech: (pg. 140) The part of a gun behind the barrel.—*Webster's New World Dictionary*

caisson: (pg. 13) A two-wheeled ammunition wagon, especially for the artillery.
—*Random House Dictionary*

canteen: (pg. 87) (1) A place outside or inside a military camp where cooked food and liquids are dispensed. (pg. 123) (2) A small metal or plastic flask, usually encased in canvas, for carrying drinking water.
—*Webster's New World Dictionary*

demi-cannon: (pg. 141) *Demi-:* Less than usual in size, power, etc. *Cannon:* A large, mounted piece of artillery.
—*Webster's New World Dictionary*

dixie: (pg. 16) *British Slang.* A pot or pan for cooking, used in the field by a soldier.
—*World Book Dictionary*

dog-robber: (pg. 87) *Military Slang.* An officer's orderly.—*Webster's New World Dictionary*

foxhole: (pg. 11) A small pit, usually for one or two soldiers, dug as a shelter in a battle area.—*Random House Dictionary*

G.H.Q.: (pg. 6) General Headquarters. *Military.* The headquarters of a commanding general in the field.—*Funk & Wagnall's Dictionary*

haversack: (pg. 80) A canvas bag for carrying rations, etc., generally worn over one shoulder, as by soldiers or hikers.
—*Webster's New World Dictionary*

impressed: (pg. 80) To press or force into public service, as sailors.
—*Random House Dictionary*

lanyard: (pg. 116) A cord with attached hook, for firing certain types of cannon.
—*Webster's New World Dictionary*

leftenant: (pg. 14) British usage of *lieutenant.*
—*World Book Dictionary*

Maginot Line: (Preface, 1st pg.) A system of heavy fortifications built by France before World War II on the border between

France and Germany from Switzerland to Belgium.—*Webster's New World Dictionary*

mortar: (pg. 17) A cannon very short in proportion to its bore, for throwing shells at high angles.—*Random House Dictionary*

noncom: (Preface, 3rd pg.) *Colloquial.* Clipped form of noncommissioned officer. *Noncommissioned officer:* An enlisted person or any of various grades in the armed forces, as, in the U.S. Army, from corporal to sergeant major inclusive.
—*Webster's New World Dictionary*

one-pounder: (pg. 60) pounder: A gun that discharges a missile of a specified weight in pounds (usually used in combination).
—*Webster's New World Dictionary*

orderly: (pg. 86) *Military.* An enlisted man assigned to perform personal services for an officer or officers or to carry out a specific task.—*Webster's New World Dictionary*

P.C.: (pg. 32) Post Command.
—*Random House College Dictionary* and Editors

pillbox: (pg. 42) A low, enclosed gun emplacement of concrete and steel.
—*Webster's New World Dictionary*

pneumatics: (pg. 24) *pneumatic gun:* a gun using

compressed air or gas as the propulsive force usually to throw dynamite or other high explosives.
—*Webster's Third International Dictionary*

regulars: (pg. 142) *Military.* Designating or of the permanently constituted or standing army of a country.
—*Webster's New World Dictionary*

rifling: (pg. 141) *Military.* The cutting of spiral grooves on the inside of a gun barrel to make the projectile spin when fired, thus giving it greater accuracy and distance.
—*Webster's New World Dictionary*

rotor props: (pg. 192) *Rotor:* The system of rotating blades by which a helicopter is able to fly. *prop:* Clipped form of propeller.
—*Webster's New World Dictionary*

sortie: (Preface, 4th pg.) A rapid movement of troops from a besieged place to attack the besiegers; a body of troops involved in such a movement; to go on a sortie; sally forth.—*Random House Dictionary*

subaltern: (pg. 2) Any commissioned officer in the British army ranking below a captain.
—*World Book Dictionary*

three-pounder: (pg. 27) *pounder:* A gun that discharges a missile of a specified weight in

pounds (usually in combination).
—*Webster's New World Dictionary*

trench mortar: (pg. 17) Any of various portable mortars for shooting projectiles at a high trajectory and short range.
—*Webster's New World Dictionary*

Vickers Wellington bomber: (pg. 1) A twin-engined medium airplane that became the standard British Royal Air Force bomber.
—*Dictionary of Aviation*

"I am always happy to hear from my readers."

L. Ron Hubbard

These were the words of L. Ron Hubbard, who was always very interested in hearing from his friends and readers. He made a point of staying in communication with everyone he came in contact with over his fifty-year career as a professional writer, and he had thousands of fans and friends that he corresponded with all over the world.

The publishers of L. Ron Hubbard's literary works wish to continue this tradition and would very much welcome letters and comments from you, his readers, both old and new.

Any message addressed to the Author's Affairs Director at Bridge Publications will be given prompt and full attention.

BRIDGE PUBLICATIONS, INC.
4751 Fountain Avenue
Los Angeles, California 90029

About the Author
L. Ron Hubbard

Born in 1911, the son of a U.S. Naval officer, L. Ron Hubbard grew up in the great American West and was acquainted early with a rugged outdoor life before he took to sea. The cowboys, Indians and mountains of Montana were balanced with the temples and throngs of the Orient as he traveled the Far East while a teen-ager.

By the time he was nineteen, he had voyaged over a quarter of a million sea miles and many thousands on land recording his adventures and experiences in a series of diaries. These were mixed with story ideas as L. Ron Hubbard began to develop his unique writing career.

Returning to the United States, his insatiable curiosity and demand for excitement sent him into the sky as a barnstorming pilot where he quickly earned a reputation for skill and daring. He set new records in motorless flight, and a number of popular articles on aviation followed, before he turned his attention again to the sea.

This time it was four-masted schooners and voyages into the Caribbean. He was later awarded the prestigious Explorer's Club flag which he flew aboard vessels he used on numerous expeditions into Alaskan, Mediterranean and Atlantic waters.

L. Ron Hubbard mixed his early adventures with an education that was to serve him well at the typewriter. While his first articles were nonfiction and based upon his aviation experience, he soon began to draw from his travels to produce a wide variety of stories: adventure, mystery, aviation, Far East action, westerns, and fantasy.

By 1938, already established and recognized as one of the top-selling authors of the field, he was requested by the publishers of a newly acquired magazine, *Astounding Science Fiction,* to try his hand at science fiction. Though educated as an engineer, he protested that he did not write about machines, but that he wrote about people. "That's just what we want," he was told.

The result was a cornucopia of stories from L. Ron Hubbard that changed the face of modern science fiction and fantasy, and excited intense critical comparison—then as now—with the best of H. G. Wells and Edgar Allan Poe.

His renowned classic *Final Blackout* was written during this period, electrifying the readership with its gripping premise of the agonies of a future nuclear war. The landmark work not only attracted vast popularity but also swirled a gale of controversy in an era that struggled to deny the possibility of universal conflict. To this day, *Final Blackout,* revealing intimate understanding of frontline leadership and the harsh realities of war, not only remains a benchmark novel for the very best in speculative fiction, but serves as a timeless beacon warning of political exploitation and excess.

Shortly after completing this masterwork, L. Ron Hubbard, with his vast knowledge of command at sea was called to combat service as a United States Naval officer.

Before World War II ended, as he, himself, recovered from wounds, L. Ron Hubbard concenrated on the task of fully researching and understanding the human condition

Over the next forty years millions of words of his non-fiction appeared detailing his remarkable researches and discoveries.

In 1980, to celebrate his golden anniversary as a professional writer, L. Ron Hubbard returned to science fiction and created *Battlefield Earth: A Saga of the Year 3000.* The epic, hailed as the biggest science fiction book ever written, quickly moved onto every national best-seller list in the U.S. and shortly thereafter was republished in fifty-three countries.

This singular feat was followed by an even

more spectacular achievement, his New York Times best-selling magnum opus, the ten-volume *Mission Earth* series—not only a grand science fiction adventure in itself, but, in the best tradition of Jonathan Swift and Lewis Carroll, a rollicking satirical romp through the foibles of our civilization.

L. Ron Hubbard's prodigious and creative output over more than a half century as a professional author has assumed the awesome proportions of a true publishing phenomenon. With more than two hundred novels, novelettes and a library of nonfiction books and published texts, and more than two hundred short stories culminating in almost a hundred million copies of his works sold in thirty-one languages worldwide—L. Ron Hubbard is without doubt one of this century's most important and influential authors.

MORE
BESTSELLERS

BY
L. RON
HUBBARD

A saga of the year 3000

BATTLEFIELD
EARTH

#1 International Bestseller • Over 3,000,000 copies in print

L. RON HUBBARD

This has everything:
spense, pathos, politics, war, humor, diplomacy and intergalactic finance."
— PUBLISHERS WEEKLY

...huge, rollicking saga...the pace starts fast and never lets up."
— ATLANTA JOURNAL-CONSTITUTION

"If you like...fast, unrelenting 'Raiders of the Lost Ark' action, then this is the book for you. It's a real page turner."
— ROCKY MOUNTAIN NEWS

The year is 3000. The future survival of the human race is at stake. This is the epic story of how one man, Jonnie Goodboy Tyler, tackles the greatest malignant power in the universe despite overwhelming odds, interplanetary strife and complex political manipulation.

FEAR

A NOVEL OF SUSPENSE

"A classic tale of creeping, surreal menace and horror... one of the really, really good ones." -- Stephen King

Fear is the hair-raising tale of James Lowry, adventuring ethnologist and college professor, who loses four hours of his life and begins to go mad as he tries to remember what happened. Hailed as one of the milestones of 20th century horror literature, this relentless tale is an unprecedented tour de force of suspense and the unforgiving power of fear itself.

Hardback $16.95